GRIM VOWS

THE ACCIDENTAL REAPER URBAN FANTASY SERIES, BOOK 6

MISTY EVANS

Beach
Path
Publishing
LLC

Grim Vows, The Accidental Reaper Series, Book 6

©2024 Misty Evans

ISBN: 978-1-964028-09-5

Cover Art by Fanderclai Design www.fanderclai.com

Formatting by Beach Path Publishing, LLC

ONE

lack, clack, clack...
We slithered through the night like a giant snake crawling toward the great Carpathian Mountains, the noise of the wheels on the tracks echoing through the train car.

The rhythmic sound, along with the gentle rocking, should have soothed my nerves. It didn't. Ancient, craggy peaks formed a backdrop outside the window, their tips spearing into the leaden night sky.

Heavy snow fell like a mask over everything. Growing up in southern Louisiana, I'd never seen so much of it or such incredible mountains.

An unsettling dread ate at my stomach. I was supposed to be the happiest girl on the planet, about to marry my soulmate in an ostentatious castle, yet I couldn't figure out why I wasn't—or why that dread had been clinging to me for hours.

Biting my bottom lip, I studied the chessboard on a slim table between me and my fiancé. The constant *clackclackclack* ticked off the seconds of my amateurish indecision. Not only was Killion a master vampire and my future groom, but he was also an expert at the game.

As we were playing strip chess and I was down to my lacy bra and matching panties, it was obvious I was not. All he'd removed so far was his tie and pocket hanky. I suspected the pieces I'd won were pity throwaways on his part, so I didn't get discouraged and quit.

Fat chance.

Chewing on my poor lip in an effort to concentrate, I studied the app on my phone that gave me various options. Killion was patient, watching the passing scenery, yet I sensed his heart wasn't in the game, either. Since we'd departed Dante's Grove on our way to Romania, he'd been distant and distracted. While I had been looking forward to seeing his homeland and his family's castle, he appeared caught in a web of memories. From what I'd gathered through our telepathic link, most weren't all that great.

My cell lost bars, making the app useless. I pressed deeper into the plush, velvet-covered seat. Our private section of the reserved compartment was at the tail end of three hulking cars. No typical European sleeper for us, this was a mini-hotel, complete with a full-size bed draped by a coverlet the color of blood and matching curtains on two square windows. Wall lamps lit the room, and we had an assortment of food and a dorm-size refrigerator that chilled my companion's necessary nutrition. The nearby cart, chained to the wall to keep it steady, contained wine and sparkling water.

Killion hadn't touched any food or drink, adding to

my worries about his emotional state. His striking profile against the wintery night on display outside the window was an artistic work of rugged jaw and prominent cheekbones. His midnight black hair had grown out in the past few weeks, and curls danced at the nape of his neck. His mouth was set tight, and the stillness he always exuded was even more pronounced.

I made the worst possible move simply to get the torture over with. I needed to call on other methods of distracting him. "Your turn."

He didn't even glance at the board. "Why are you throwing away the game?"

I gestured at my lack of clothes. "I'm freezing and jet-lagged." We'd flown his private jet from Louisiana to the East Coast, then boarded a larger, but still private, one to cross the Atlantic to England. After refueling, we'd arrived at a small airport in Romania and then got on this train to journey into the mountains. The group of friends traveling with us was entirely made up of supernaturals. My family—entirely mundane and nonmagical—along with my best friend—also in the mundane department—would be joining us a few days before Christmas to witness our vows.

Our current transportation was part of the discreet system they preferred, yet it did have a few human passengers as well. I'd seen a woman dressed in a woolen coat and boots that had seen better days cross herself when her gaze landed on us as we'd entered. Although I, too, was anything but mundane, I was feeling the fallout from the extreme time change and the hours spent in the air. "I'm too keyed up to concentrate."

The violet eyes he turned on me were so dark they appeared black in the dim light. His expression was unreadable, though I knew it well. From our bond, he could tell I was truthful yet not confiding everything. I swallowed and stared back, refusing to let that intense gaze intimidate me.

He swiftly took my queen and cleared the vintage walnut board of the remaining hand-carved pieces. Outside of the king and queen, the chess pieces sported ugly creatures with horns, fangs, and claws. They had odd names and looked like they'd come from a mythical story. "Which is it? Are you keyed up, or are you jet-lagged?"

Busted. "Both...?" He gave me a stern look. "Hey, I'm unique, as you are so fond of reminding me."

The corner of his mouth quirked, an acknowledgment of the statement as accurate. He'd teased me about my oddness repeatedly since our first encounter. An inside joke of sorts. That tiny movement loosened the muscles in my shoulders, and I breathed deeply. Even with our connection, there were times when it was impossible to get him to show any emotion.

His gaze went to my bare skin and lingered there, then to my lips. "Perhaps we should put your energies toward other pursuits."

He pushed mental images into my mind of things he wished to do to me. Lust coursed through my veins, dragging me from my earlier worries. The chill I'd felt vanished, replaced with warm desire. "I did lose the match, so I guess that means..." I slipped off my seat and around the table, sliding in next to him. "You win."

He cupped the back of my head, cradling it as he brought his lips to mine. His other hand rested on my hip, drawing me close. "I did, indeed."

Slowly, he explored my mouth, the heat of his powerful body and his magic enveloping me. The desire between us rose higher, but rather than me luring his mind away from his awful memories, I knew he was doing this to distract me instead.

I drew away, trembling from the kiss and determined to clear the air. "What is it? What aren't you telling me?"

His lips firmed, a muscle jumping in his jaw. He rested his forehead against mine. Started to speak, then hesitated. "Everything will be fine."

The crystalline forest outside the window had a blue tinge, thanks to the waxing moon shining nearly full and round. I ran my fingers across his chin and down his neck. "It will," I assured him, the dread returning, thick and burdensome. "Tell me what's bugging you so I can make sure of it. We're partners, remember? We work together and share our worries."

He grabbed a blanket to wrap me in. "There is nothing you need to worry about."

"I'm worried about *you*. I didn't realize returning to Graven Castle would cause you this much distress."

He tucked the cover around my shoulders. "Neither did I. You must understand, that place... It is as if we are going back in time. The castle, the forest, the people. It's nothing like you've encountered. Every stone, every tree, every waterfall has its own story. The myths and legends humans tell have been convoluted over thousands of years, but many of them have the seeds of truth."

He'd said that to me before when discussing his heritage. Vampires were far older than popular fiction or human myths claimed. His ancestry, in particular, came from a different dimension and dated back to a time our current world knew nothing about. "Like dragons."

His voice lowered. "You must never divulge my secret. There are those here who would experiment on me if they knew."

Being the last descendant of a purebred line of vampires, he embodied dragon magic. The beast inside him was kept in chains, but I'd seen a glimpse of it and knew the immense force it took for him to keep it from breaking free. "No one will ever hear it from me, and there's no way I'll let anyone experiment on you. Ever."

A thoughtful smile tugged at the corner of his full lips. He wasn't prone to sighing, but I sensed an internal one all the same. I may have sucked at chess, but I was the greatest grim who'd ever lived. My magic was still new to me, yet it was a deep well that had saved me multiple times.

"The staff at Graven have only known me by my given name." In supernatural circles, true names held great power and were only shared with specific individuals. "Because your family and friends will join us in a few days, I have requested all household members refer to me as Killion. No master and no talk of my true name."

Outside of one member of his nest traveling with us— a vampire named Pennyworth who'd been with Killion's family since before Killion had been born—our entourage only knew him by his chosen French moniker. "That's who you are to all of us," I assured him. "Not the child you were when you lived there."

He was as unique in the Undead world as I was in the Reaper one. His conception had been unanticipated by his parents—a vampire father and his human bride. While Killion and his first wife, also human, had conceived a boy, both had died centuries ago during an influenza outbreak. His son, Marco, had never demonstrated any Undead tendencies. The elite vampire blood in Killion's system had not transferred to him. "I am not, and yet..."

There was only one other living vampire-human hybrid, and Mason was part of Killion's nest. The two were close, and I was glad. No one could replace Marco, but Mason was a good kid, and I knew Killion's grief over his son's demise was lessened by having him around.

"Yet, what?" I brushed my fingers over his chest. "None of us ever truly leave our pasts behind. I know your father was a jerk, but he and your mother loved you. They loved each other."

"My father's brutality was directed at me only when he thought I needed it. I was... incorrigible in many ways. That's not what's bothering me. It's—"

A sharp knock on the stateroom door interrupted the rest of that statement. Too late, I felt the prickle of Moss' vampire magic in my blood. I'd been so focused on Killion, the limo driver had snuck up on me. On my mate, too, it seemed.

Killion left me to answer the door separating us from the three other cabins in this car. "What is it?"

The train was slowing. With the door open, the

annoying clacking was louder, and my teeth grated against each other. Without shifting to see Moss' face, the dread in my belly froze, knocking against the weight of my fear. I slipped on my clothes.

"Sorry, Master." Moss hesitated, then pushed the words out. "There's been a..."

"A what?"

I stood on trembling legs as a ghost floated into the compartment, confused and angry. "Where am I?" she asked. "Why am I in here?" She speared me with a set of horrified eyes, a trickle of grayish blood soaking her neck and trailing under her wool coat's collar. "You have to help me!"

As a grim reaper and employee of Soul Management Group—the divine organization that handles life, death, and everything in between—it's my job to do exactly that. Two marks were visible at her carotid, making it easy to guess the cause of her death. "Someone's been murdered," I said to Killion, reaching for my clothes. "And it looks like a vampire did it."

TWO

We passed through the front of the car, our Undead companions opening the doors of their smaller sleepers as they felt their Master's distress. Probably mine, too, since the channel between us was fully open.

Killion's enforcer, Katarina, was video-chatting with Harlow, his second in command at home in Danté's Grove. She pressed her phone to her chest as she filled her doorway. Her reception must have been better than mine. "What's up, Master?"

Moss kept ahead of us. "A human is dead in the center car. Appears to be homicide."

Killion motioned at her to follow us. "I'll inspect the body. See if you can pick up the trail of the killer."

Her bangs moved as she lifted her brows. She said a quick goodbye to Harlow.

The car rocked, and I felt as untethered as the ghost floating between me and Killion. "He's one of them," the specter snarled at his back. "*Vampir.*"

Pennyworth and his partner, Omwee, watched us from their compartment. "And us?" Pennyworth asked.

"Stay put," Killion ordered. "I'll summon you if I need you."

The butler glanced at me as if asking if I agreed. He and I had grown close during the past year, and his protectiveness of Killion was a trait I shared. He'd been a member of Killion's household for hundreds of years and knew Transylvania, the legends, and the people better than the Master himself. I nodded my assent—if this went sideways and any of our companions were suspects, we might need him to run interference.

In the middle car, passengers gathered around the body sprawled in the aisle between two booths. This car was for those traveling short distances who didn't want or need sleeping quarters. Each side held a row of cubicles with tables, and riders stored briefcases, purses, or backpacks under their seats or on the wire shelves overhead.

Most of the occupants peered over and around the high-backed seats, their frightened voices rising and falling above the clacking of the wheels. Two hovered about the corpse and glanced up when we drew near. One, a woman in a thick coat and trousers, shrank back at the sight of Killion. The other—a balding, overweight man in coveralls under a dirty jean jacket—appeared ready to cry. "Are you the guard?" he asked the master vampire, his accent British. "I swear on the Queen's grave, I 'ad nothin' to do with it."

The female skittered to her seat, fumbling for something in her bag crammed next to her. She found it and hid her hands under the table. "He's no guard," she spat. "*Voivolde. Drăculești.*"

Killion had warned me about the superstitions that hung over the country like fog on the mountain range. I'd read much about the history of Transylvania and Vlad the Impaler, on whom Bram Stoker had based his Dracula character. The fictional version held few truths yet hit a trigger with many, both past and present.

While the majority of Romanians believed the House of the Dragon, also known as the Basarab Danesti, and its most famous ruler, Vlad, had rescued them from the Ottoman Empire, there was much mystery and an ongoing fear of vampires. The tourism industry benefited greatly from this, capitalizing on Bran Castle, which Vlad had never lived in but had been made famous by the novel.

I was unsure of the translation of her first word, but I knew the second. *The House of Dracula.* Dracula being a another name for dragon.

The train was slowing. I stepped between her and Killion. He paid no attention to her, and I didn't know what she was hiding under the table, but I was pretty sure she knew he was the real deal.

Not good.

She shrank back under my stern gaze before I faced the others.

Killion didn't answer the man's question, asking his own instead. "What happened here?"

"Was looking for a seat, is all, mate. She 'ad her head down on the table, sleeping. I asked if I could share the booth, and when she didn't respond, I figured it must be all right." He rubbed his face with a beefy hand, his breath smelling of alcohol. Drinking on this public train was prohibited, but I'd bet a month's wages he had a cask inside his jacket. "A bit later, I noticed the blood."

A copious amount covered her side of the table and dripped onto the floor.

Killion studied it, his nostrils flaring delicately. "How did she get from her seat to the aisle?"

"I shook her shoulders," the man explained. "Tried to see what was wrong. I 'ad to pull her out."

The ghost hovered about, crying softly. "I was supposed to get married next weekend. *Quelle horreur.*"

She was French. "Who did this to you?" I asked. "Is he here?"

The British man glanced at me, blinked, and shook his head as if trying to figure out if he was hallucinating—or I was.

Killion drew his attention with another question, and while he was distracted, I bent over the body.

The specter's head snapped to the left. "Oh no! He's coming!"

"Who?" I asked.

She vanished.

The gal who'd returned to her seat snarled under her breath, her accent Romanian. "Leave her be! You have no right to touch her. The guard will be here any moment."

All the more reason to make my examination quick. Moss moved to block her while I studied the neck wound.

The blood had slowed to a trickle. One of the puncture wounds had hit her carotid, yet glancing around, I saw no arterial spray. The other was off-center, missing the vein entirely.

Sloppy for a vampire. Were they in a hurry?

The ghost appeared again. "My fiancé! He'll be so distraught!"

My eyes caught on a carpetbag shoved under the seat. I needed to calm her down and get some answers. "What's your name?" I asked.

"Madeline," she hiccupped. "Friends call me Maddy. I have to hide! He's coming."

"Who?" I asked. "The killer?"

She disappeared again.

So much for getting a name or description of our suspect. If she didn't reappear, I'd have to reach out to my boss, Death, and ask for his help. I needed to know if her soul contract was up. If not, she was what we in the death biz called a shade—someone who had died before their time. Being a reaper, I would have to harvest her earth-bound spirit to keep her from lingering on the human plane.

Maybe Maddy's belongings would give me a clue. When I caught her eye, Katarina, hanging back and watching those around us, stepped forward. I used my chin to point toward the carpetbag while I leaned closer to Madeline's body, patting her pockets. There was a handkerchief and ticket stub. No cell phone or identification. This close to her blood-soaked clothes, my superior nose picked up the heavy odor of metal.

Blood smells coppery, and there was plenty of that on her and in the air, but this was different. Heavier.

I drew the odor deeper into my nostrils. I knew that

scent—the same as my sparring partner's finally-edged sword. Katarina loved her blades, and this smell was of steel mixed with the faintest layer of soap.

I sat back on my heels, confused. No weapon was left behind, and the smell was heaviest at her neck. I'd never met a vampire with metal incisors or one who would use soap to clean steel. I *guess there's always a first.*

The train came to a stop. "What are you doing?" the woman in the booth demanded of Katarina. She was peering around Moss' massive form.

I rose to my feet, adding myself to the shield blocking her view as the enforcer became invisible. Katarina extended her magic to the bag, and it did, too. Vampire magic flooded the car along with her glamour, and no one noticed her disappearing act. Before I could ask our irascible passenger if she could corroborate the Brit's story, the front door flew open, and two men stepped inside.

A frigid blast of winter air swept into the car along with them. The conductor shouted at everyone to move back, dismay in his voice. "Return to your seats immediately," he said in Romanian.

Or something like that. I was as good at translating Romanian as I was at chess.

The other man was dressed in a gray uniform. His eyes narrowed on the dead woman and hardened when he noticed our proximity to her. At least he spoke English. "What are you doing there? You're contaminating the scene."

"He's a detective," I blurted, pointing at Killion and smiling. I hadn't even stopped to think—it just came out.

The guard barked a command, this time in his native

tongue. I didn't understand, so I smiled wider. "No one has touched the body except for him." I shifted my finger to the heavyset drunk. Distraction was always a good move. Sometimes, playing a bumbling American worked, too.

The guard's hair was as dark as Killion's and had enough product in it to make my friend, Nita, jealous. He filled out his uniform with hard muscles and broad shoulders, the tight set of his jaw causing a tic in his cheek. He glared at Killion, and for a split second, I swear I saw something like...recognition?

The air between them snapped with a ferocity that caused the hair on the back of my neck to rise. They sized each other up like two fighters in a ring. Killion gestured at the drunk. "I'd start by questioning him."

"Should I stake him?" The seated woman whispered to the guard. "He's a *sweet one*."

I whirled, shocked by her offer and confused by the term. She seemed all too happy to insert herself into this. "Did you see who murdered this woman?"

She flinched back. The rider across from her shifted closer to the window as if trying to distance herself from all of us. "I... No," the nosy gal said, lifting her chin before she pointedly spoke to the guard. "I was sleeping."

"Then stay out of it," I ordered. "This is a serious matter, and the officer has a long night ahead of him, interviewing all of the passengers and handling this poor woman's body until we reach the next town. He doesn't need hysterical folks like you creating chaos."

If nothing else, my rhetoric scored points with the man. He sized me up as if I might be a legitimate ally, then seemed to discard the idea. His attention returned to Killion. "What kind of detective?"

Killion removed an elegant business card from his jacket and addressed him in his native tongue. "Killion Reveux. *Privat anchetator*."

The guard took the card, gave it a cursory glance, and stuck it in a pocket. "I'll take it from here. Return to your seats. I'll be with you soon."

Killion gave a nod. He drew me away from the crowd. The stake-happy woman stood and called us names, cursing in Romanian. When I started to reply, Killion kept me from turning and lowered his voice. "Let it go."

Moss had his back to us, watching the crowd. I wondered if they all had stakes hidden on their persons, but that was ridiculous. Even the few supernaturals among these humans wouldn't attack us.

Would they?

I allowed Killion and Moss to escort me to our private quarters. Whatever had happened and whoever had done it, we had miles to go before we arrived at our destination. This trip was supposed to be about my wedding, not a ghost and her murder. Becoming embroiled in this affair was asking for trouble.

Too bad trouble *always* seems to find me, no matter where I go.

THREE

Katarina dumped the backpack's contents on the table where Killion and I had played chess. Pennyworth and Omwee had joined us. We watched as she rifled through the items, snagging the passport. "Madeline McDonald, thirty-four, lives in Paris but lists Ireland as her birthplace."

"She told me she's engaged—was, anyway." I thought of all I'd cataloged about her. "There was no ring on her finger, though. Did somebody steal it? Could that be the reason for her murder?"

No one had an answer.

"How did you discover her?" Killion asked Moss.

The burly chauffeur crossed his arms. "I was in the dining car reading when the lights went out. I waited for them to come back on, and when they didn't, I got up to check on you."

"They went out?" I glanced at Katarina. "Ours didn't. Did yours?"

"Nope. I've had cell trouble," she said, "but we expected that due to the mountains."

Moss shrugged. "They did in the other two cars. When I entered the passenger one, I noticed that the air temperature was at least ten degrees cooler, and I felt... weird."

"Weird how?" I asked.

"Like Death was breathing down my neck." He shuddered visibly, uncrossing his arms and shifting his weight. "I almost turned around and fled back to the dining car, but I smelled blood. The lights came on. That drunk started shouting. He jerked the dead gal out of the booth and everyone went looloo."

Killion glanced at me. "Why did you volunteer the information about my services?"

"We needed a reason to be snooping around the victim." I pointed at the small wooden stake among the purse's contents. "Does everyone here carry those?"

Pennyworth adjusted his nightcap and shook his head. "Not locals who've been born and raised here."

"Unless they're hunters," Omwee added.

Pennyworth flicked a finger at it. "Marketing vampires is a tourist trap. Selling such trinkets provides those businesses with plenty of revenue."

"Hunters?" I asked. "You mean, like Buffy?"

The vampires in the room all rolled their eyes.

Killion scowled. "Not only vampires. The Vaneti hunt all supernaturals."

The sides of the miniature stake were so smooth it looked plastic. "Are the Vaneti like that Van Helsing dude?"

Another eye roll from all but Killion. From him, I got a patient smile. "Similar. The Vaneti are real and highly dangerous mortals. They've been around as long as anyone can remember and pervade all continents in search of their targets."

"Even America?" I asked.

"In the bigger cities," Omwee told me. "Which is why so many of us avoid such places."

"Is it possible Madeline was supernatural?" I hadn't scented anything other than human on her, but Killion had taught me never to assume the obvious. "Could she have been carrying the stake to protect herself from them rather than another supe?"

"Doubtful." My fiancé studied the stake, his hackles bristling over its intended use. "She shows no signs of having magic, and the Vaneti do not attack in public. They work covertly."

"She definitely ran afoul of someone," Pennyworth said softly.

"Vampires don't attack in public, either." Katarina tossed the passport on the pile. "At least, not smart ones."

Killion addressed me. "Did you smell her attacker on her?"

"Did he smell like whiskey?" Moss added.

Disappointed I couldn't appease them, I shook my head. "Her blood presented as normal. I did detect a metallic scent around the wounds on her neck. They were staggered, by the way, not lined up like a vampire's precise strike at the vein." I happened to be all too familiar with such things. "Weird, right?"

Two things that fell into the weird category.

Everyone stared at the table as though it might produce answers. The train began to move again, giving an abrupt lurch.

"Perhaps it wasn't fangs that made the punctures," Killion said. "However, the attacker may be playing on the fears of tourists and locals alike by making it appear so. The guard will be here soon to interrogate us." He gestured for Katarina to collect the items and replace them in the backpack. "Make sure that turns up where he can find it, but does not implicate us. Everyone watch your back. Stay alert, and make note of any supernaturals you encounter, as well as those who may be *vânători*. Vaneti," he clarified for me. "While they don't typically strike humans or carry out their hunts in public, we aren't taking any chances."

A hunter, maybe more than one, was on this train? Odds seemed high. "The woman in the booth across from the murder seemed pretty anxious to stake you," I said to him. "Could she be one?"

He chuckled. "She was far too outspoken and eager. True *vânători* move in the shadows and hide in plain sight as ordinary citizens. She's fueled by fear, which makes her someone to watch, but she's no hunter."

"I assume there are a lot of them here," I said, watching Pennyworth assist Katarina in stuffing the backpack. "The Vaneti?"

Killion glanced out the window, the passing landscape disappearing into a wall of thick forest. "Enough."

He turned away; I felt his worry slipping through the channel connecting us.

My gaze slid to the window. It seemed odd that we

were moving again so soon, but then, we were in the middle of nowhere, climbing steep terrain in winter. It wasn't as if a crime scene team from the nearby town could get to us. "When the guard asks, should I tell him about my observations?"

"No," he replied. "Tell him you checked for a pulse and realized you couldn't help the woman. You said a prayer for her—nothing more."

I had said a quick prayer for her. After working in the morgue for several years, it had become second nature to do so. "I'll do what I can to get her ghost to talk to me. She can tell me who we're looking for, and we can point the guard in their direction."

"You were quick to volunteer my services."

It sounded accusatory. "Like I said, we needed a reason to be futzing around her. It was the first thing that popped into my head."

The others' attention ping-ponged between us. He held still, the noise of the train filling the tense moment. "I don't wish for us to become entangled in this situation more than we already are." *Understood?*

I didn't like his tone. "While I agree it would be best to lay low, I can't. If her spirit hasn't crossed over, she was killed before her soul contract was up. Now she's a shade. She falls under my jurisdiction, and it's my responsibility to help her move to the afterlife."

"Are you sure her contract isn't up?"

"She wouldn't linger if it was." He knew that. "What's going on here? You raced out of here with me when Moss came to tell us, and now you're peeved that I volunteered you as a detective to assist with the investigation."

His features hardened. "He's not just any guard, Chloe."

The dread came slithering back. Was the man supernatural? Had I missed that fact?

I scanned my memory of him and his scent. I hadn't detected anything more than his dislike of Killion, of all of us, but that was because of the situation, right? We'd invaded his territory and were suspects on his list.

There was something more. Something...personal. Killion hadn't shut down our channel, but had gone radio silence. "Killion." I touched his hand. "Who is he?"

His jaw clenched, the power radiating off him heating my skin. "He's a Danesti."

The bomb dropped, except I wasn't sure why that was a problem. I shifted closer, searching his face. "As in the House of Vlad? A vampire?"

"The opposite, actually."

"A hunter?"

The others scrambled out of the car, Moss giving me a *you're on your own with that pool of quicksand* look as he closed the door behind them.

"A hunter of a different kind." Killion braced both hands on the table. "He is my sworn enemy."

FOUR

A knock at the door made me jump. Everyone, including my friends, Aurora and Andy, filed back inside, filling the compartment like packed sardines.

Andy and Aurora wore night clothes and had messy hair. Aurora stifled a yawn, rubbing her eyes. "What in the name of the goddess is going on?"

"A murder, a shade, sworn enemies." I shrugged. "The usual."

"If that's all..." Andy grinned and ran a hand through his long strands of hair, trying to tame them. "I'm going back to sleep. This jet lag is a killer."

Killion stopped him before he got to the door. "Because you're a member of my party, you'll be questioned by the royal guard who's on the train and investigating a murder. Tell the truth about being in your compartment asleep, but keep your status as a supernatural to yourself."

Aurora narrowed her astute green eyes at me. Her

witchy aura flared with a protective magic shield, and her Irish lilt grew thicker. "Murder, you say? The guard suspects *you*?"

The shield was a vibrant blue and warmed my skin. "A human female, and not me specifically, but possibly a vampire."

Her attention shifted to our Undead companions. "And?"

Katarina straightened, indignant. "And what, witch? You think any of us would feed on a human and kill her?" She made a disgusted sound and pointedly glared at Andy. "Teeth marks and blood could point to a multitude of supes."

His lip curled. "What reason would I have to kill her?"

"The moon is nearly full." She jutted her chin to the window. "Maybe you couldn't control your basic dog."

"Racist, much? I'm a shifter, not a common werewolf."

"I'm no more racist than you and your witch," she snarled, showing fang.

"Enough." Killion cut the air with a hand. "Bickering is unproductive." He told Andy and Aurora what had happened in a brief sentence or two. "None of us did it, but whoever did is still on the train. Let's focus our efforts on pointing the guard to him or her, shall we?"

"Why did that woman call you a 'sweet one?'" I asked. I'd forgotten until now.

He sighed, exasperated. "It's an archaic term used in the eighteenth century when vampire sightings became *en vogue*."

"Folks believed using the correct term would call a vampire to you," Aurora added, "so they used phrases like 'I saw an uncle' or 'I saw a sweet one.'"

"Weird," Andy said.

Another item in my weird column.

My phone rang with the theme from the movie *Halloween*. I snatched it up to silence it and saw a text from Diego, my apprentice back home. *Help*, it read.

One word. Since he was new to the grim reaper gig, I felt compelled to reply, but since he cried for help more often than the kid in Aesop's fable, I quickly typed out: *Busy. Call Death.*

I was supposed to be on vacation. Plus, I was thousands of miles from him. There wasn't much I could do, regardless of the degree he needed me.

A brisk knock at the door got our attention. We exchanged a glance as the royal guard called, "Open up. I need your official statements."

Killion nodded at Pennyworth and he straightened his nightshirt before taking a breath. Technically, he didn't breathe but needed to steel his nerves. His official butler face slid into place as he opened the door, stepped back, and motioned the guard inside. "Welcome. Please join us."

He strode in with the confidence of a man with a badge, but due to the crowd, didn't make it more than two steps. He had the air of one who knew his strengths and weaknesses, and even as he took a headcount, he didn't so much as blink. He did another sweep, noting every possible weapon and hiding place. I'd seen Killion do the same when he entered a new environment or met someone he didn't know.

"I'm Officer Danesti." He rocked on his heels, finally meeting and holding Killion's gaze. "They all belong to you?"

Aurora raised her chin and bawled her fists. "We don't *belong* to anyone. At least, I don't." She gestured between her and Andy. "We're friends attending Killion and Chloe's wedding."

Andy placed a hand on her lower back. While I couldn't hear his thoughts, I recognized the gesture. *Down, girl.* "We'll bug out. Leave you guys to talk."

Danesti raised a hand. "Where were you when the woman was killed? Here?"

Aurora tugged her robe tighter. "We were asleep in one of the smaller units you just passed. We only woke when we heard everybody in here talking."

The guard's eyes bore into each of them. My instincts flared—he was scanning them for a reason. To see if they were supernatural? Did he have that skill? I sniffed in case I'd missed something and sent a trickle of my magic out to inspect him.

"Can anyone vouch for your whereabouts at the time of the murder?" he asked my friends.

Andy moved her to his side, ready to shield her. Not an easy feat with us packed in so tightly. "We were sleeping, like she said."

"So that's a no." He eyeballed Moss, Pennyworth, and Omwee, questioning them similarly about their whereabouts and alibis. Moss received the most consideration since he'd viewed the scene right after it had occurred. He held the guard's intense scrutiny without a flicker of nerves.

The whole time, I felt like I would crawl out of my skin. Mentally, I asked Killion about him, and he confirmed the man was human, yet my instincts refused to be appeased. He was a threat, pure and simple.

Finally satisfied, Danesti closed his notepad. "I've already confirmed your story with those present, both in the dining and passenger cars."

Moss snickered, annoyed. "Then why the third degree?"

"Witnesses can be wrong, see what someone wants them to see." He turned his focus on Katarina in her short black skirt, a red sweater that emphasized her cleavage, and thigh-high studded black boots. "And you? I suppose you were sleeping, too."

"I don't sleep. I was on the phone with a friend."

If Danesti suspected she was a vampire, that seemed to check a box on his list to confirm it. "I'll need to see your calls and speak to your friend."

My phone went off again, the creepy theme song filling the cabin. "Sorry," I said. Diego, who went by Die, was calling this time. Something was up. I squeezed past Aurora. "I really need to take this."

"*Domnișoară*," Danesti said, voice hard. "I insist you stay."

Omwee moved aside to let me pass. I didn't look back as I exited. I shut the door as I answered. "What is it, Die?"

"I'm, like, so, so sorry, Chloe." His goofy voice was muffled and sounded far away, static interfering with his words. "I'm at a Christmas concert and..." His voice cut out. "...this ghost..." Loud static blasted my ear, and I jerked the phone away and waited for it to quit. "She's ruining...I can't get her to talk to me."

He was bordering on whiny. "Call Death," I shouted into the phone. "Make him help you."

"I didn't want to bug you...he hasn't responded...she just shut off all the lights. I don't know what to do!"

It was his first time soloing, and I felt bad for him, but this was the job. No matter how much training we had, every non-compliant, or ghost in this case, was unique and sometimes required out-of-the-box thinking. The only way to learn was by jumping feet first into the fire. "Can you get close enough to show her your scythe?"

We carried magical blades that were compact and lightweight but packed a punch. We didn't typically have to swing them, only show them to our target. They appeared as something the non-compliant soul, or ghost, loved. It helped relieve their fear of us and acted like an invitation to touch the blade so they could be on their way to the afterlife. "Um..."

"Um, what?"

"I didn't bring it." Before I could chastise him, he hurried to explain and the connection improved. "I'm supposed to be off tonight to attend this concert. It's my first Christmas! I mean, you know, *not* in someone else's body." Previous to becoming a reaper, his spirit had bounced around for centuries in other people's meat suits. "I really love this holiday. Hal is with me. I knew he'd love the music."

As he rambled, I rubbed my temple, trying to think of

a way he could take care of the ghost under the circumstances. While he had his psychopomp, they were both too inexperienced to handle this on their own without the blade.

Static assaulted my ear again. The only reason we were still connected had to be due to reaper-to-reaper magic.

"You have to call Death," I insisted over the noise of the wheels and the poor connection. "If he doesn't show up, there's nothing you can do."

"You're sure? I don't think he's happy with my work, and if I can't handle this, he might fire me."

He would, but not until I was back on duty. "I'll talk to him and smooth it over. Don't worry. You won't get fired." I would have to make sure of that. "Look, I have to go."

"How is it there? Is the castle cool? Are you excited about the ceremony? Gee, I wish I could see it."

"We haven't gotten to Graven yet. I'll take plenty of pics to show you—" The connection broke.

I leaned against the wall, peering at the four compartments across from me. Like the Hogwarts Express, they were lined up on the right side of the car with this narrow passage on the left. The doors to all four units were closed, and three had the shade drawn on their tiny window. The one directly across from me was Katarina's. She'd left hers up and I could look through the small sleeping space to the exterior window.

Movement in the woods caught my attention, and I stepped across the threshold to peer at the landscape rushing past.

A pack of wolf-like creatures ran among the trees, racing the train. Their heads were malformed, incisors elongated to twice the average size, and their coats were covered with snow and ice. Their fur rippled like needles as their muscled bodies sprinted through the snow.

"What in the reapers...?"

The train jarred, the sudden movement sending me into the compartment. My foot caught on the narrow bench seat, and I catapulted forward, my hand smacking against the icy window.

As I watched, the alpha, still racing us, swiveled his head and stared straight at me.

FIVE

I watched as the pack kept pace, dodging tree stumps and rocky outcroppings. We had to be going forty to fifty miles an hour, and wolves only ran in short bursts above thirty.

At least, that's what I thought. I was only a few weeks away from taking my boards to become a full-fledged veterinarian for domesticated animals. Even if I'd studied wildlife medicine, this group would be an outlier. Not only did their appearance suggest they were supernatural, so did their speed and grace.

From above the trees, a streak of light rent the air and a rip in the sky's fabric opened. I blinked at the group that emerged, riding equally unusual mounts down an invisible incline. The male leader was bare-chested with long silver hair flowing behind him. He held a crossbow nocked with a gleaming arrow, and his stead was part horse and something else unknown, with black fur, curled horns, and flat wings that rose and fell in great pumps through the air.

Mesmerized and horrified in equal amounts, I watched as he and his companions bore down on the unsuspecting pack.

He rode bareback without reins, using his knees to guide the grotesque steed. His cohorts brandished spears, swords, and darts. As they grew closer and closer, I put a hand to my mouth, holding my breath. I couldn't blink, couldn't look away as the scene unfolded.

"Oh, no." Madeline's ghost was back. "He's come for me!"

"Who?" Watching the head rider, I saw him release the arrow from his bow at the exact moment the alpha wolf cleared a copse of trees. It flew true, nailing the pack leader in his neck and sending him tumbling.

And then, as one, the riders and wolves disappeared. Just...vanished.

I reared back, stumbling over Katarina's luggage. I whirled toward Madeline, but she was nowhere in sight. The train lurched, and I sat hard on the bench seat. "What just happened?" I murmured.

The nearly full moon was now a garish red. The trees and snow reflected the color, making the world appear bathed in blood.

Yet there was no evidence of what I had witnessed. The train chugged along, hauling us farther and farther from the scene.

"Madeline," I called, swallowing hard. "Talk to me. Tell me who killed you. Explain what you meant about him coming for you." She'd been terrified of the hunters. Their leader could not be the same being who'd administered the puncture wounds to her neck. Could he?

I had no idea who or what he was or what those creatures were. I'd encountered my fair share of otherworldly specters, but these were outside my realm of knowledge.

The faces of Killion's chess set flashed in front of me. None of those monstrous faces matched the creatures the hunters had ridden or those of the wolves. However, the sensation scraping against my spine and demanding an explanation suggested there was a connection.

I was either hallucinating or something—dare I say it? —*weird*, was ensnared in those woods, playing out that scene over and over. It sometimes happened with ghosts who became trapped in a specific time and place that couldn't move on. Like Madeline would be if I didn't manage to get her spirit to cross to the afterlife.

She didn't appear, and I returned to the rear compartment. Danesti stood near the door, about to leave. He chastised me. "In case you do not understand how serious this is, I will place you under arrest if you leave again without my permission."

I was shaking and didn't respond. Shuffling past Moss and the others, I gripped Killion's arm. He sensed my dismay and took my icy hand. "Are you all right?"

Leaning into him, I inhaled his reassuring scent of warm caramel and old libraries. "I am now." His magic wrapped around me like a toasty blanket. To the guard, I said, "I apologize. It was work-related, and I needed to take it. The person filling in for me is in a difficult situation."

His disapproval didn't wane, nor did his determination. "What is it that you do...Miss..." He glanced at his notes. "Frost. You're Chloe Frost from Danté's Grove, Louisiana, correct?"

"I'm a veterinarian and own a clinic. A vet had an emergency and needed instructions."

This didn't seem to fit with his notion of me. He paused, frowning. "I will need the name and number of the person who called you."

"Why?"

"To verify your statement."

All I needed was for him to call Diego. All the ways that could go bad raced through my mind. I started to argue, but Killion squeezed my fingers.

Cooperate. Against my better judgment, I withdrew my phone, punched in Diego's number, and hit the speaker button. "Fine. We can talk to him right now." To my surprise, the connection went through, and the blare of his phone on the other end filled the cabin. Before Danesti could argue, Die picked up.

Hurriedly, I said, "Sorry, I know you're in the middle of a tricky situation with that guinea pig, but I need you to tell the royal guard on the train who's with me *right now* that you called me for instructions on how to handle Hal's..."—I thought fast. Did Danesti know anything about rodents? I went with something common and universal—"ringworm issue. You're on speakerphone, by the way." *Please get the hint and play along.*

"Stop," the guard ordered. He snatched the phone and muted it. "Do not lead him into saying what you want him to." He was about to address Die when Death and Madeline appeared, startling me. Neither was corporeal; they floated right through the others.

My companions didn't see them, but a harsh tone emitted from the phone when Danesti put it to his ear, causing him to jerk back.

Thank you, I mouthed to Death.

"You have work to do," he said, glowering. He pointed at Madeline. "Get your scythe and harvest her now."

The sound of hooves striking the roof caused me to glance up. Madeline shrieked. "Please don't let him take me!"

Then the train braked hard, and we all went flying.

SIX

I smacked onto the table and fell into Katarina. Regaining my footing, I realized everything had come to a stop, frozen. All those around me were in various sprawled postures, their features stuck in surprise.

Shaking Katarina, then Killion, did nothing; I was the only one able to move.

On the roof, I heard the clatter of hooves again and Madeline's wail. I shoved Danesti from the door where he had fallen. Where was Death?

The air outside the compartment was bitter cold, and the moon was still blood red, but there was no wind and no sounds coming from the woods.

To my left, an attached metal ladder led to the roof. The icy bars bit into my skin as I grabbed hold and climbed. A foot slipped, but I caught myself before I fell. My ribs, which slammed into the metal, didn't thank me. I'd be bruised later.

Regaining my footing, I hauled myself up, up, up. As

my head cleared the top, I stopped. The hunting party was gathered there, and my stomach cramped as their horrible, otherworldly magic hit me.

The smell of rotting wood and damp moss invaded my nostrils. I swallowed the ball of fear lodged in my throat and forced myself the rest of the way onto the slippery canopy.

Halfway down the car, the leader, whose bare skin and silver hair glowed, held an arrow out to Madeline. "Touch it," he ordered.

"What are you doing?" I yelled. "Leave her be!"

His gaze slid toward me, but hers stayed locked on his weapon. His silver eyes, as dead as the unnatural stillness around us, hardened. "She is mine."

I needed to break her hypnotic stare at the arrow. In my haste to reach her, I slipped. My arms flailed, and I danced on the icy surface, crying out as I nearly slid over the side. The hunting party simply watched.

Steady once more, I kept my hands out to aid my balance. I was breathing hard, puffs of clouds forming in the air as I spoke. "I don't know who you are, but she's not a piece of property. She's not yours, and I'll take care of her. It's my job. She needs to move on to the afterlife."

His head tilted as he sized me up. I couldn't place him, nor could he reason out who I was. "Her grandmother was a moss maiden. Her blood says so."

Where had Death gone? I inched closer, reaching out slowly and carefully to the ghost so as not to startle her. The other riders tensed, coming to attention en masse like soldiers anticipating a fight. They fingered their weapons, their eerie supernatural eyes locking on me.

Were they readying themselves to defend their leader? Did he need such a defense?

My teeth chattered. Mentally, I called to my boss. *What is going on here? Who is this nut job?* "I have no idea what a moss maiden is or what that has to do with this." Even if I touched Madeline's shade, I had no scythe or psychopomp—both were back home. Regardless, I *did* possess the magic to send her to the afterlife, but it would take a careful approach. If I spooked her, she might disappear forever. "She was murdered before her soul contract was up, and I will make sure the killer is brought to justice. But she can't stay on this plane." *And whatever weirdo stuff you plan to subject her to.*

Thanks to my reaper job, I'd learned about assorted creatures who used ghosts and harvested souls for all sorts of spells, sorcery, and conjuration. Necromancy was a particular kind of black magic, and while the ability to wield it ran in my veins, it was unnatural for others to do so. Raising the dead, harvesting souls, trapping ghosts...it all upset the universal balance, and Death and Soul Management Group were big fans of balance.

The hunter's nostrils flared, and his eyes narrowed, something clicking into place for him. "You," he muttered. "Why are you here?"

His accent was unlike any I'd ever heard. It was deep and resonant yet as bitter as the sharp night air. He spoke English, or at least it translated inside my head as such.

I shivered hard, unaccustomed to the frigid temperature. "Take your friends and leave."

He laughed, full-bellied, as if my order was a joke. As if *I* was. Then all humor fell from his face, the hard lines of his cheekbones highlighted by some internal frost. He stepped forward, invading my personal space and glaring down at me. He had to be a good foot taller than I was and his irises were ice daggers. "This is *my* territory. You don't belong here."

"You're not taking—"

One hand snaked out and gripped my neck, cutting off my words. I scratched at his bony fingers, my feet pedaling on the slippery surface under them. Only his grip kept me from skidding off.

Madeline gasped, and his cohorts exchanged shocked glances. He shook me like a rag doll. "I will throw you from this train if you interfere with my hunt."

My eyes bugged out, and black spots appeared at the edges of my vision. While Death was ignoring my telepathic plea, I sent an SOS to Killion, then kicked at the being holding me, my boot nailing him in the shin. He didn't so much as flinch.

Death appeared with Ghost in his arms. My psychopomp, in her canine form, barked and showed her teeth to my attacker. "Release her," Death commanded.

The ice daggers swung, bored, to my boss' face. "Why?"

"Show respect. Now."

There was no quarter in Death's voice. His directive rattled inside me, vibrating my very bones. It seemed to have a similar effect on the others, and the members of the party slid from their mounts and took a knee, bowing their heads.

To him?

No—to *me*.

Their leader didn't so much as blink. He peered deeper into my eyes, searching for something. "Is she..?"

"The one and only." Death stroked Ghost's fur, soothing her. "What are you doing here, Eriling? This isn't your rightful domain."

The finger vise opened, and I fell. I hit the glazed metal roof and scrambled for purchase as my body slipped dangerously close to the edge. Unfortunately, the only thing remotely grabbable was Eriling's leg. It was as solid and unmoving as a tree trunk. He glared down at me until I righted myself into a sitting position.

Gasping in lungfuls of air, I rubbed my throat and wished for my scythe so I could slice the jerk in two with it.

"Please don't let him take me," Madeline whined in my ear.

"I have dominion over the Forest Fae," Eriling snarled, "wherever they might be."

"True," Death said. "But not on a train in the middle of...?" He glanced around, taking in the landscape. "Right, Romania. Harvesting a shade here is her job." He pointed at me. "She also has seniority, in case you've forgotten."

The flinty daggers speared me again as Death helped me to my feet. My voice came out scratchy. "You're...a... grim?"

His naked chest, with its layers of odd necklaces, expanded. "I am *the* psychopomp."

Ghost barked. I coughed and patted her head. Madeline hiccupped and disappeared. What timing. "Psychopomps escort the dead to the afterlife, not hunt their ghosts down like prey."

He grinned, bone-white incisors sharp. "You have gone soft, Grim Zero."

If Death hadn't held onto my arm, I might have fallen for real. "You know who I am? Who I *really* am?"

He smirked. "This incarnation is a disgrace compared to your original."

I removed Death's grip and stepped into Eriling's personal space this time. "I have compassion for the dead, and I make sure they're respected and feel safe. You're..." —I motioned at his outfit—"frightening and disgusting. If anyone is a disgrace to the Reaper Team, it's you, buddy boy. You need a makeover in the worst way—your looks *and* attitude." I spoke over my shoulder to Death. "Does SMG offer sensitivity training? This guy needs it."

From Eriling's expression, the term perplexed him, but he shook it off. "You've cost me a soul tonight, Grim Zero. I will not forget it."

He mounted his stead in an easy leap, using his legs to urge it into the sky. The others followed, shooting disquieted glances my way before they disappeared into the fog.

My neck felt bruised. I whirled on my boss. "What in the reapers just happened?"

Before he answered, the train catapulted forward. I landed on my belly, snow flying into my face and blinding me. Take two on me scrambling for anything to keep me from tumbling off the now-moving car.

A hand gripped mine, and I was hauled up. Strong arms wrapped me in a bear hug, and I blinked snow from my lashes, discovering I now stood on the narrow platform between cars, safe inside Killion's hold. "Why are you out here?" he called over the clacking wheels and ferocious wind.

The glacial air stung my face, stealing my breath. "Can we...go...inside?"

Death was nowhere to be seen, but Ghost danced at my feet. I was glad to see her—now she could be part of our nuptials. Inside, the others were gathered around an unconscious Danesti, lying where I'd left him on the floor near the exit.

I held Ghost while Killion rubbed warmth into my arms. "Is he okay?" I asked through chattering teeth.

Katarina shrugged. "Hit his head. What do you want us to do with him, boss?"

Pennyworth disappeared down the hall into his and Omwee's sleeper. Killion regarded our visitor. "I'll heal him once Chloe explains why she was on the roof and how Ghost got here."

I gave them the short version, accepting a cup of warm tea when Pennyworth returned. Killion wrapped a blanket around my shoulders, and I allowed Ghost to sniff around as I answered questions.

"Eriling?" Aurora frowned at the mention of his name. "As in the Elf King?"

"Such a legend does not exist in our culture," Killion said. He addressed me. "He claimed he was a psychopomp?"

I nodded. "*The* psychopomp. He knew Grim Zero."

Aurora arched a brow. "The original conductor of souls. How cool is that?"

"He's anything but cool." I rubbed my throat. Killion studied the bruising and placed his hand on one side. His magic invaded my bloodstream, and I knew I'd be healed shortly. My grim power would do the trick on its own, but he liked feeling needed. I just liked his touch. "He's vile. I saw him earlier along the forest where he shot a wolf-like animal chasing the train."

Killion moved to the other side of my neck and glanced at Aurora. "As in The Wild Hunt?"

She nodded, her face still showing some type of awe.

"I don't know what that is," I said, "but they were hunting a pack of creatures."

She appeared delighted to explain it to me. "The Wild Hunt is a spectral horde of hunters who sweep through the forests in winter. They are associated with the Underworld, and anyone found outside at night around Yule might spot them." She spoke to Killion. "They exist under one name or another in many cultures, and there's plenty of folklore about the extent of their powers. Most claim that it's best to stay inside or they'll snatch you."

I shivered, even though I was no longer cold. "He claimed Madeline had moss maiden blood." I finished the tea. "What does that mean?"

"Moss maidens are part of the Forest Fae. They are a quiet, elusive bunch," Killion said, handing the empty cup to Pennyworth. "One of the oldest but most secretive of Fae. They reside in forests and wooded areas such as these." He gestured to the window.

"Like literally reside *in* them," Aurora added. "They

can merge with trees, streams, and even rocks. Some cultures refer to them as dryads, nymphs, or tree spirits."

Madeline chose that moment to show herself again. "Help!"

I shucked off the blanket and handed it to Aurora. "What's wrong?" I asked the ghost.

"The man...the one who killed me." She floated to the door, peering down the way. "He's about to jump from the train!"

SEVEN

My heart leaped into my throat. While Killion could sometimes see ghosts, nobody besides myself and my psychopomp seemed to notice her. She jetted through the side of the train and vanished from sight.

"Come on!" I gestured for the others to follow as I raced past the sleeping compartments. "Our killer is about to get away!"

Throwing open the door, I gripped the railing as the wind and snow hit. The train car where Madeline had been killed was only a few feet away, but the metal was slick, and the moon had been covered by clouds, rendering the night dark as pitch. Tiny balls of sleet stung my face, and my eyes watered.

A hand gripped my waist, and Killion propelled me effortlessly across the expanse and into the next car. Our sudden arrival caused most passengers to glance up as we packed the aisle between the seats. Seeing it was us, most of them quickly looked away.

Ahead of me, Madeline's ghost sped past the site where she had been murdered and toward the dining car. Her body was nowhere in sight, but her blood still lay in the aisle, congealing. Why no one had covered it or cleaned it up, I couldn't be sure. I stepped over the pool and caught sight of our suspect through the minuscule window in the upper part of the connecting door. He wavered outside on that platform. His face was out of view, but his bulky coat was familiar.

"What's going on?" Danesti asked from behind me. "What are you doing?"

Somehow, he was on his feet and moving with us, probably thanks to one of the vampires in our group. I reached back and grabbed his arm, yanking him over the blood. "Our suspect is getting away."

He rubbed the back of his skull and pried his arm from my grip. "Who?"

"The man who murdered Madeline." I pushed him toward the exit. "He's out there on the platform about to jump!"

The woman who'd given us grief earlier came out of her seat, eyes wild. "She's lying!" She pointed a stake at Killion. "He's the killer!"

Pandemonium broke out; passengers who agreed with her came to their feet yelling. None of them had stakes, so she was my priority. Danesti barely glanced at her as he threw open the door.

Madeline floated to the right of the man, wringing her hands. He was the drunk fool who claimed he'd found her body, and he reared back as the guard laid hands on him. Madeline shouted in French, and the two men wrestled with each other. I worried they would flip off onto the tracks together, but Killion's magic snapped out like a claw, gripping both of them.

Moving in front of the woman, I held up a finger. "This is your last warning. Sit down and be quiet, or you'll find that stake in your own heart."

She gasped but did as instructed, glowering at me. At that moment, I didn't care. I rushed to the opening where Killion stood, trying to keep Danesti and the killer from going over the side. His magic formed a barrier, blocking them in. However, they were tussling so hard, I was afraid they might break through it.

Behind us, some of the passengers gasped as Danesti's foot slipped off the edge of the metal. My own heart spiked. I started reaching for him, but Killion was there, grabbing the men by their coats and hauling them inside.

The three tumbled to the floor, taking me down with them. We landed in the blood, and more passengers gasped. I tried to disentangle myself, the breath forced from my lungs by the weight of the drunk man on top of me.

He bared his teeth, the same hatred I'd seen in the woman's eyes shining from his. He no longer appeared the least bit inebriated. Had it all been an act? "Vampire whore," he spat.

Killion and Danesti yanked him off of me, and I wheezed in a shaky breath. "You know," I said between gulps, "this idyllic train ride through the Romanian countryside has been anything but romantic."

Killion released the man to Danesti and helped me to my feet. "Are you all right?"

Was I? "I need something stronger than tea when we get back to our cabin."

Danesti frowned at my bloodied clothes. "How do you know this man is the killer?"

Well, this was awkward. I glanced at Madeline, who had stopped crying and looked relieved. She began babbling. "He said he was friends with Robert, my betrothed. Said Robbie had sent him to give me a necklace. He offered to put it around my neck, but instead, he...he..." She hiccupped. "You know." She pointed to the man's coat pocket before touching her wound. "It's in there. The thing he used."

"Check his pocket," I told Danesti. "The weapon that punctured her carotid is in there."

The guard did so, finding what resembled brass knuckles. Two of them had sharp points on the end that resembled fangs. They'd been wiped clean of blood.

"Bet he didn't get those at the souvenir shop," I muttered.

Danesti held them in front of the man's face. "This is what you used?"

Our Brit didn't even spare him a glance. "I've never seen that before in my life. Someone must've planted it on me."

"He's lying," Madeline said.

Danesti gave me a raised brow. "I suppose that's possible."

Ire burned in my stomach. I was tired of this farce. "I haven't even been close enough to spit on him. The ghost of the dead woman told me."

People around us drew back, and Killion rubbed his eyes. I'd done it now.

Danesti looked amused. "Is that so?"

"Yes, I talk to ghosts, and she says he did it and was about to jump from the train to get away."

The man snickered. "She's unstable," he said, minus his heavy accent. "You can't believe a word she says."

Danesti sighed; whether from exhaustion or irritation wasn't clear. Whatever it was, it mimicked Killion's emotions, which pulsed along our channel. "I need to borrow a private cabin to interrogate him."

"You can use mine," Katarina volunteered.

"I'm innocent," the man insisted.

The train rocked, and I leaned against the woman's booth, gripping the edge to steady myself.

Killion took my elbow, scanning my face. "We'll wait for you in ours," the master vampire told the guard. "I must get Chloe food and drink. It's been a rough night."

"Tell him about my fiancé," Madeline shouted at me. "Tell him about the necklace!"

I relayed the information to Danesti, who looked uncomfortable and skeptical at the same time. "And where is this piece of jewelry?"

I glanced at Madeline, and she pointed to the man's front pants pocket. I did the same.

He tried to fight the guard's dive into it, but Moss stepped behind him, and our killer went still as stone.

Danesti removed a raw gemstone pendant on a long gold chain. The stone glowed red in the train car's interior. "I'm certain you'd know if someone slipped this into your pants, so save the excuse about being a setup," he told the man. "Let's go." Danesti shoved him toward the door, ignoring the passengers' raised voices. My shoulders slumped in relief. I glanced at Madeline and was glad to see a satisfied expression on her face.

"You need sleep," Killion murmured in my ear. "You're dead on your feet."

I didn't argue. After the trip, the murder, and the confrontation with Eriling, I felt off. Unfortunately, I knew I couldn't rest until we got off this blasted ride. "A warm drink and some food will help."

He nodded, motioning for Moss and Katarina to go ahead of us as he took me by the hand to lead me out. Just as I started to follow him, the woman behind me muttered in Romanian. My protective magic flared a bit too late—a sharp, piercing pain hit me between the shoulder blades.

My body locked up. I tried to scream and found I had no air. The agony drove all the way through and into my chest. My lungs wouldn't move, and in my ears, my pulse beat loud for three beats and then...

Nothing.

Passengers screamed. Killion caught me as I fell. Blackness soaked my vision as it tunneled down to a point. All I saw before everything went blank were my beloved's violet eyes.

EIGHT

When I came to, my spirit floated above my body. I was in bed, a bloody stake tip protruding from the front of my chest.

Ghost jumped and barked at my ghost.

That woman killed me. If I could have, I would've marched out and ripped her head off.

Except I couldn't do much of anything. Moss and Katarina were holding an enraged Killion back from doing what I couldn't. He swore in his native tongue and charged for the door. It took everything they had to keep him from tossing them aside.

Pennyworth and Omwee stood like linebackers, blocking the exit, and Aurora and Andy fussed over my corpse. Aurora chanted a spell under her breath, and I watched her magic weave around the walls like vines, keeping everyone imprisoned.

Killion's irises had gone red, his features pure vampire, and I floated over to comfort him. He could see my spirit. "I'm okay," I insisted, although I was far from it.

"While I'd love for you to remove the stake from my chest and put it in hers, we have enough problems without adding her murder to them."

He seethed, fangs on full display. "You are *not* okay. You are, in fact, *dead*."

Moss and Katarina couldn't see me but understood who he spoke to. Aurora moved forward, eyeing my phantom form. She could see ghosts most of the time. "Chloe? Goddess be." She put a hand to her mouth and shook her head. "I didn't realize you'd succumbed. I thought your heart was still beating."

The stake had stopped it, ripping into the flesh of the four quadrants like a drill, but I was Grim Zero. I'd died and came back more than once. "Pull it out, and I'll be good."

Killion yanked his arms from Moss and Katarina's grip. "It's done massive damage. You'll bleed out before I can staunch the wound."

Aurora peered at my physical presence on the bed. "I can cast a spell to slow the flow when you remove it. It will cause a stasis state so that you can heal her."

His eyes still glowed red, but his fangs receded, and his features became more human. Katarina and Moss stayed on alert, as did Pennyworth and Omwee. Killion planted himself in front of my spirit, a stone that wouldn't be moved. "I can't lose you."

His voice was strangled. My throat tightened. "You won't. I can resurrect myself, remember?"

"You have a limited number of times you can do that, and we don't know how many you have left."

Aurora tsked. "We've discussed this, Chloe. You don't

have unlimited lives." She touched Killion's arm. "Trust me. Her heart hasn't stopped completely. I can feel it. I'll slow her blood, and you can heal her before she dies."

He searched my face, and I gave a reluctant nod. It was worth a try. "Go for it."

Moss and Andy sat me up per Aurora's instructions. Katarina pinned my thighs to the mattress, and Aurora chanted over my head, holding a hand in front of my heart and another behind it. Killion listened, his fingers curling around the stake's blunt end, waiting for her enchantment to kick in. When she gave him the cue, he placed his free hand on my shoulder to brace me, then pulled.

Nothing happened. My grim magic was attempting to heal the wound, and I could feel how it had braided the wood into my tissues. "Harder," I told Killion. "You need to get it out now."

He yanked. The wood resisted.

"Again," I said, feeling a touch of alarm. "Give it all you've got."

He seemed reluctant but nodded. This time, he braced his feet on the bed and both hands around the wood. Using all of his vampire strength, he wrenched it free.

It had turned dark from my blood. Aurora raised her voice, the spell injecting her healing magic into the jagged hole left behind. At the same time, Killion poured his into me, heating the skin and bone surrounding the puncture. It began to close, and he glanced at my ghost. "Return to your body."

With that command, I felt my heart contract, trying

to recover. Circulation was restricted, however, and it felt as if my chest was tearing in half with every beat. The injured muscle thudded hard, trying to do its job, and I gasped. All eyes flew to my corpse's face.

Killion dropped the stake on the bed and thumped my back. "Come on, Chloe."

I couldn't decide if I was technically dead or not—I'd previously experienced actual death, as well as this in-between shade-like phenomenon. This time, it felt... different. Like neither of those events.

Another check went in my weird column.

A tug in my solar plexus yanked me toward my physical form. The bond Killion and I shared created a silver thread between my body and spirit. I mentally latched onto it, using it like a tether, and pulled my specter into my human shell hand over hand.

It worked. My chest expanded on a ragged inhale, and a sharp pain resonated inside my rib cage. My eyes flew open, and I was once more alive and breathing, although it felt like fire blazed inside my lungs.

Everyone sighed with relief. Killion gently brought my back to his front, hugging me close. It took a minute before I could speak, my limbs weak and my pulse sounding too loud in my ears. The room swam in shades of monochrome until my vision cleared. "Well," I said. My voice sounded as though it were underwater. "That was...not fun."

Aurora made several motions with her hands, and a heaviness about my head and shoulders lifted. Breathing became easier, and the blood in my torso, freed from her spell, gushed into my legs and arms. While I still felt drained, I could lift a hand to my chest, the torn material of my shirt bloody, but the open puncture sealing itself.

With a few parting words, the others left, and Killion laid me down, securing the blankets around me. He placed the stake in a plastic bag and set it outside the door for Danesti before bringing me a glass of his blood.

All I wanted was to sleep, but he forced the rim to my lips and made me sip. I was no vampire, but his blood had properties that could boost my grim healing and expedite the process. I dozed off in his arms and didn't wake until he shook me sometime later.

We'd arrived at the train station, and under Danesti's orders, we waited until the passengers had disembarked and scattered before we exited our car. He had Madeline's murderer and the woman who had attacked me under arrest but drew Killion aside before we piled into the waiting SUVs.

My hearing wasn't as acute as a vampire's, but I could still make out most of what he said. "I need a formal statement from your fiancée. Are you sure she doesn't need to go to *camera de urgență?*"

The ER. Definitely not.

"I have taken care of her," Killion told him in a matter-of-fact manner.

He didn't ask how. "The passengers will talk. Word will spread." He shot a glance at me from the corner of his eye, then focused on the line of vehicles. "I believe our culprits may have been working together to scare them more so than commit murder. A ruse that went wrong."

"Scare the passengers for what reason?"

"There has been a steady resurgence in fearmongering over the past few years, recruiting common folks to hire security guards and enroll in training to protect themselves from...things that go bump in the night."

"I see. Preying on people's fears to boost business is an age-old and prosperous tactic."

They stood silent for a heartbeat, then Danesti placed a cap on his head. "You've all been through enough for tonight. I will let your statements about this last incident go until tomorrow, but I will need them. If, that is, Ms. Frost wishes to bring charges against Ms. Carmilla?"

Killion's attention sharpened. "Carmilla?"

Danesti nodded. "An unusual name, yes? Especially for someone who claims to hate sweet ones?"

Unspoken communication passed between them. Killion pointed to Danesti's pocket where the guard had stuck Killion's business card. "My number is on there. Will you need us to come into town?"

"Would you rather I come to you?" There was a slight challenge in the question.

Killion drew on thick gloves. "I would not."

Danesti chuckled. "Figured as much." He withdrew Killion's card and studied it. "Graven Castle? Of course. I should have recognized you, *Monsieur Reveux.*" Again, a hint of challenge with a hefty amount of contempt. "Pretending to be French these days?"

Killion offered a chilling smile, the tips of his fangs showing. "*Mais, bien sûr.*"

"Do you have internet at your castle?"

"*Pourquoi?*"

"I can take your statements that way. Save us both time and effort."

I sensed Killion was torn. He glanced at me, and a shiver ran over me at the concern in his gaze. "I'll consider it," he said.

I stopped shivering, the warmth only he could give enveloping me.

Danesti tipped his hat. "I'll be in touch."

In the parking lot, Killion introduced us to the Undead drivers who would take us to the castle. Pennyworth seemed to know all of them, and while they greeted him warmly, they studied me with vague indifference and lifted their noses in thinly veiled dislike at Andy and Aurora.

"None of that," I said to them, gesturing to the witch and shifter. "You don't have to like them, but they're my friends, and you'll respect them while they're here."

Killion tugged me close. "You'll respect *everyone* in this group. They are all under my care and protection."

The three chauffeurs bowed their heads and said in unison, "*Da, stăpânul meu.*"

Yes, my master. I grinned and rubbed my arms through my thick wool coat. That was better. "Can we go now? I'm freezing."

Moss opened the door of the lead SUV. It was the length of Killion's limo back home and just as black. I climbed in with Ghost, and Killion slid in beside us. He sent the rest of our group to the other two waiting vehicles.

"Are you comfortable?" he asked, looking me over.

My chest still ached, and I longed for one of Pennyworth's fabulous meals and some alone time with my partner. "I'm tougher than you give me credit for."

"I know exactly how tough you are. Let me take care of you anyway."

I snuggled into him. "Who is Carmilla?"

He hesitated, then placed a hand over mine. "That is the name of the title character in a gothic vampire story written by Sheridan Le Fanu nearly three decades prior to Bram Stoker's *Dracula*. Carmilla is an aristocratic vampire who preys on and seduces women in the book."

"Wow. I've never heard of it."

"Most have not. A curious thing for your attacker to have as her surname."

"You think she's using it as an alias?"

He stared out the window at the passing city, which had few lights on at this time of the morning. "I think it is a message. Of what, I'm unsure."

I rubbed my chest through my jacket. Seemingly unaffected by the frigid temps, Ghost circled my lap three times and settled in for a nap. My eyelids felt too heavy to keep open. I fought it, wanting to stay awake and ask more questions about everything—the Forest Fay, Eriling, The Wild Hunt—but all I could manage was to stifle a yawn.

"It's quite a few miles yet," he told me. "Rest. I'll wake you when the castle is in sight."

"I don't want to miss anything." My body betrayed me, my head dropping onto his broad shoulder even as I said it. "I can sleep once we get..."

I didn't finish the sentence.

Dreams came and went like the wind. I was in a

tunnel, running from Death. Next, I was in an under-ground cave, searching for someone with violet eyes. Then, I was barefoot in the snow, the forest closing in on me as the sound of hooves gave chase.

In each, my chest burned with fire.

In the one with the forest, I glanced down and saw the pointed end of the stake protruding from my heart. I latched onto it and tried to remove it, but my hand came away slick with blood.

"You can't escape the truth," a voice that sent goose-bumps over my skin said. *"You can't escape me."*

Hot breath touched the back of my neck, and I whirled to find Eriling looming over me. I stumbled away, kicking up snow, but smacked into the trunk of a tree. The impact drove the stake deeper, and I spewed blood. Even in the shadows of the thick forest, the drops shone ugly on the white snow between us, marring its purity. *"Never,"* I spat. *"I will never be hunted."*

He stepped forward, holding up a gleaming arrow and smiling into my face. He was brutally handsome and absolutely terrifying. *"You already are."*

NINE

I woke gasping for air. Ghost jumped from my lap, and Killion took me by the shoulders, searching my face with a furrowed brow. "What is it? What's wrong?"

I coughed, ripping open my coat and shirt. My grim tattoo glowed orange against my skin. I scratched at it as if I could rip it out. "The hunter..." I sobbed. "Eriling. He was in my dream. He's coming for me."

Killion drew my hand from the ink. "You've been under too much stress. You're overwhelmed, and our experience on the train resurrected old fears and ancient memories. Your subconscious is trying to work through it, but you're safe. I won't let anything happen to you."

"He was in my *dream*," I insisted, trying to gain control of my emotions. No one could keep me safe in those, but I would not allow them to rule me. "It felt so real."

He rubbed my back in slow, comforting circles.

Pushed a whisper of his heat over my shoulders. "You always have intense nightmares."

Something about this one felt different. I couldn't find words to describe it. "The snow, the stake. My blood." I shuddered.

He asked me to give him the details, so I did, stumbling over the words. I couldn't seem to paint an accurate picture of the dream, and just replaying it in my head made my spine tense.

Ghost nudged my hand. The cage around my ribs unlocked. "I'll be all right in a minute," I told her.

"Are you sure?" Killion asked.

One minute, he was asserting I was safe; the next, he seemed uncertain himself.

Outside, the first rays of dawn turned the horizon lavender. Our caravan wound its way up a steep mountain. Thick woods rolled out on one side, a carpet of snow-capped tips flowing down the slopes. On the other, the terrain climbed into the morning mist.

The straight tree trunks reminded me of prison bars, and I forced myself not to give into the cage that wanted to lock up my chest again. "Yes, of course. I'm better already." I sipped hot cocoa from a travel mug, forcing it down my tight throat. "As long as I have you and Ghost, I'm good."

He was quiet, a leader on the battlefield assessing his soldier's condition. "Once we are at the castle, you'll be more settled."

I wasn't sure if he was trying to convince himself or me. Even as the potent fear of the nightmare subsided, I felt edgy and ill at ease.

Absentmindedly, I ran a hand through my hair. My fingers came away wet as though I'd only just been outside. I stared at their tips, imagining I could see snowflakes there. The strands were probably still damp from leaving the train and climbing into the limo, but the chill of the forest had sunk into my bones. "How much farther?"

We slowed for a switchback turn, and he pointed out the window. "Look."

The indigo sky was fading away reluctantly. To the north, rising like shark teeth from the mountain mists, the peaks of a stone castle emerged. Clouds floated above the turrets, the last of the twinkling stars overhead winking out.

Why did that seem like a portent?

As more of it came into view, I realized Graven Castle was massive. Even though I'd seen pictures of it, none had done it justice.

Built into the side of the mountain during the Middle Ages, it resembled a creature daring us to draw near. Its arched windows watched our approach above the stone wall surrounding it. Giant dragon statues perched on each tower peak, wings out as if ready to take flight.

A single ray of sunlight snuck over the mountain and landed on a section nearly hidden from view. As the SUV turned toward the bridge to take us across a frozen river, I could hardly take in the multiple connected buildings, varying roof lines, and the eerie glow that oozed from every slab, chimney, and door.

I drew back. "What is that?"

His voice sounded perplexed as he answered. "Graven Castle."

"No, I mean the glow. It's like St. Anne's, except it's..." The abandoned Catholic church was a magical oddity in Dante's Grove. It actually existed in two worlds —the seen and unseen. Both good and evil. He used it for training and interrogations. This place had that unnatural magic to it, and as I squinted at the castle again, the mere sight of it made my skin crawl. "Unwelcoming."

He placed a hand on my arm, calming and reassuring. "You can see it?"

The bridge was made of the same stone as the castle, and the tires rumbled across it, vibrating the entire vehicle. It was so narrow that as I snuck a glance over the edge of the wall, I could see the river below. I had the uncanny sensation of needing to get out of the car and run.

What is wrong with me? "Is it a spell?"

"A protection ward. Dragon energy. My father created it centuries ago to hide us from our enemies. It repels anyone with ill intent."

So why was it repelling me? "That's one intense security system."

"Does it bother you that much?"

He knew it did but was as confused as I was about why. My tongue felt thick, my mouth dry. "Any chance you can lower the degree?"

His reply was strained. "Possibly, but I'll need time to research how. For now, I'll shield you from it."

Instant relief relaxed my shoulders, his familiar energy wrapping me in a bubble. I sighed into him and even laughed when Ghost placed her paws on the window ledge and wagged her tail.

We exited the bridge and stopped in front of the towering iron gates. They opened without any action on our part, sensing their master had returned. We drove through them and a second walled area before entering the courtyard proper.

Pennyworth had drawn me a map with the major sections of the castle and grounds labeled. I'd snapped a photo for my phone and studied it for hours before our trip. A paved, circular drive led to yet another gated sector, blocked by soaring wooden doors. Once again, the entrance opened as if on autopilot, the metal hinges groaning as the panels swung wide to reveal the interior castle grounds.

The dragon's power lessened here, and the glow vanished from my sight. The vehicle stopped in front of the main entrance, a set of stone steps leading to the building's grand entrance.

The driver parked and opened Killion's door. Killion tugged me out with him, and Ghost joined us. He took a deep breath, expanding his chest while the faintest of smiles played on his lips. He was home, and I tried to call up my initial excitement about seeing this place. About spending Christmas here and marrying him in such a regal setting.

If only my pulse would stop skipping over itself and my fight or flight response would calm the grim down. Even with his bubble taking the edge off the repulsion ward, I had the urge to hightail it out of there as fast as my feet would carry me.

Run, Grim Zero warned. *Death awaits.*

Her voice in my head didn't startle me as much anymore, but the cryptic warning annoyed me. *Not running. Go back to sleep.*

The others exited their vehicles and crowded around, oohing and ahhing over the impressive structure. While certainly not ostentatious or luxurious, it was awe-inspiring. I'd known it would be impressive, but I'd also thought it would be more majestic rather than scary.

Nope. Total creepy medieval vampire castle.

I took my own deep breath, forcing my unsettled nerves to relax. *Of course, it's scary.* I simply hadn't expected to be repelled at the sight of it when I got up close.

"This is grander than I imagined," Aurora said, sidling up to us. "I can't wait to see the interior, can you?"

Ghost barked in agreement. I forced a smile, although I knew it faltered. "Can't wait."

"What's wrong? You look like you've seen a ghost." She laughed at her own joke, poking me in the ribs.

Reapers be reaping, I sure hoped there weren't a bunch of spirits inside. I made a big deal of picking up the dog, so I didn't have to look her in the eye. "My stomach is off, that's all."

"Probably because you got staked," Andy supplied.

"Probably," I agreed. A flare of color in my peripheral vision caught my attention. I turned, my gaze drawn upward to a window in the front tower. A curtain swayed, suggesting someone had been watching us, but nobody was there.

A crisp breeze ruffled Killion's hair. He turned to us,

arms outstretched. "Welcome to Graven Castle, my home."

He mounted the steps with a flourish, and we trailed after him. At the double doors, he paused and placed a hand on a nearby stone under the lantern. The fire inside burned without any source other than magic.

The iron designs of the hinges twisted into intricate patterns that writhed and danced in the flickering light. I blinked, not sure if it was real or my imagination.

My breath caught as the stone under Killion's palm, along with those surrounding it, shimmered in a multitude of colors. They undulated and spread out from the center.

He removed his hand, and the stone cracked open. A giant golden eye stared at us.

"Great goddess," Aurora breathed, hand going to her chest.

"Cool," Andy said, grinning.

"Holy reapers." I stepped back, clutching Ghost tighter. "Is that a dragon eye?"

Killion's smile deepened. "*Bună, vechi prieten.* Hello, old friend."

I swear, the entire place vibrated. It was as if the dragon *was* the very stone, wood, and iron that comprised the building. Still rippling with colors and light, the edifice released a resonating bass *thrummmm*.

A response?

"Bite me," Katarina piped up. "It's not going to eat us, is it?"

Pennyworth rolled his eyes. Moss chuckled.

The doors creaked open, and Killion gestured us

across the threshold. "Not if you behave," he said, that faint grin still in place.

"Did you just wink?" I asked, incredulous.

The smile widened. He tugged me forward. "Come."

The Middle-Ages vibe of the exterior was absent inside. Marbled floors and an impossibly high ceiling met my gaze. Tapestries and paintings hung under spotlights along the walls, and a grand staircase rose on one side to a balcony that overlooked the formal foyer.

Several Undead servants dressed in black and white attire—were lined up at the base of the stairs. All stared straight ahead, stiff and expressionless. One of the males stepped forward and bowed. "Master, it's good to have you home."

The others bowed as well, and Killion nodded. "It's been a long time." He introduced all of us, and our luggage was taken upstairs. As we removed our coats, and those, too, were hustled off into the depths of the place, Pennyworth engaged each of the remaining staff with personal greetings.

"My home is your home," Killion told us. He took my hand to draw me up the staircase. "Avoid the dungeons unless you have a strong disposition, and stay on these grounds. Many forms of danger lurk outside the gates."

"No can do," Andy said. "I'm an alpha. Anytime I enter another alpha's territory, I have to make my presence known and explain why I'm here. Aegenwulf is expecting me to meet with him and bring a peace offering."

Killion paused. "Arrange for a driver to escort the two of you to the shifter's headquarters," he ordered Moss.

Moss gave his master a *kill me now look*. Andy made a *no way* motion with his hand. "I have to keep the peace, and bringing an Undead into Aegenwulf's personal domain will do the opposite."

"You shouldn't go unescorted," Killion told him. "The Vaneti are everywhere, and because of what happened on the train, they'll be alerted to our arrival."

Aurora slipped her arm through Andy's. "I'll go with him."

Killion looked distressed, but I patted his chest. "She's as good as any Undead bodyguard."

Moss grunted in argument, and Katarina snorted. Aurora lifted a brow—an unspoken threat in her eyes.

The vampires trotted up the stairs, suddenly eager to get away. "Time for bed," Katarina said.

Moss was on her heels. "See you at sundown."

That settled, we left the others to find their chambers. Ghost, who typically loved everyone, was standoffish with the maid who was assigned as my attendant and followed a few steps behind us. "We'll be fine," I assured her. "No *attending* needed."

Her dark eyes sought her master's, and Killion dipped his chin in confirmation. "I'll take care of her for now, and she will call for you when she needs you, Thana."

"*If* I need her." Which I didn't plan on. "Thanks, anyway," I said.

She curtsied and receded into the shadows of the hall. "Yes, Master."

"Are you going to tell me about the dragon?" I asked as we climbed.

"It is a dragon in spirit only. A guardian."

Like the beast that lived inside of him? I could tell he didn't want to discuss it, so I let it drop for the time being.

He drew Ghost and me through many passages and down halls. We stopped at a brightly lit conservatory in a separate wing from the main house. For the first time since we'd arrived, my mood lifted. "What is this?"

"My mother's atrium." He glanced up at a canopy of tree branches, the top ones touching the windowed ceiling two stories high. Butterflies danced around a riot of colorful flowers and the air was sweet with their perfume. "She was gifted with plants, and this was her sanctuary from the gloom of the castle, especially in the winter months. I thought you might enjoy it."

I browsed the aisles, touching herbs, houseplants, and flowering bushes. "And the tree? What kind is it?"

"A magical one. You won't find any like it in the real world."

Ghost ran the curving pathways, barking at the butterflies who dipped and soared around her. I chuckled at her antics. "It's beautiful." *So different from the rest of this place.*

"Any time you need a break from the stress of planning the wedding, escape here."

I smiled at his handsome face, and I saw how it relieved some of his worry. Weak winter light bled in through the glass panels but seemed to avoid him. I touched his cheek. "And you? Where did you find sanctuary in this ginormous place when you were growing up?"

A rare play of emotions tightened his features. "How did you know I needed one?"

Even with our telepathy and soul bond, I never saw all of him, but I'd guessed about a few things after he'd mentioned his father was a violent, brutal vampire. While Killion bore no physical scars, I sensed there were others, far deeper and lasting. His vampire blood would have healed any physical abuse, but nothing could heal emotional trauma.

"I met your dad, remember?" It had been a few seconds when I'd touched the family ring and been transported to a large hall full of vampire warriors while his parents, seated on a raised dais, overlooked the gathering. Killion was nearly an exact physical replica of his father, but I knew he was nothing like him. "King of the Romanian Undead. Scary fellow."

"That he was." He toyed with his ring. It no longer transported me through time and space, but I still avoided touching it. "He is gone now, and we are here. Let's not discuss him, okay?"

Before I could comment, he ushered me from the inviting atrium and carried me up a curved set of stairs to a tower where our bedchamber was ready and waiting.

TEN

The apartment was luxurious and faced west, so it was still in shadows. Someone had left flowers and finger foods in the outer receiving area, and started a fire in the bedroom hearth, turning down the covers. The ornate frame had four posts with velvet material strung between them.

Ghost jumped on the bed and settled down.

"She acts as though she owns the place." Killion chuckled and drew me close, playing with a strand of my hair. "We are finally alone."

His power caused a ripple of excitement under my skin. Although we'd had a private compartment on the train, it hadn't felt that way. In this place, there were probably plenty of out-of-the-way rooms where nobody would look for us. "Seems like it's been days."

He brushed a knuckle across my cheek. The fire popped and sizzled. "Are you glad you came?"

Was I? I was wrapped in his bubble, yet, I feared

what might happen if I lost it. What the castle—what the spirit dragon—might do to me.

I rose onto tiptoes under his assessing gaze and kissed him. A butterfly kiss, soft and teasing. "My place is always with you."

His body went still with its usual intensity. He typically acted as if he hated being teased and flirted with; I knew differently. After three hundred years, he'd had many conquests, but I was different—I was his *incatusa sufletum*. His bonded soulmate. "What's mine is yours. I realize you may never feel entirely comfortable here, but this is your home now, too, should you wish it."

It seemed like a dream. I was about to marry a very wealthy, handsome man who owned a castle. His life—*this* life—was about to be mine. Completely different from the world I'd grown up in.

A fissure of the earlier dread crept into my stomach.

My mind struggled to grasp the enormity of what I was about to do. I'd planned to fall in love with this place, but here I was, feeling unwelcome by its guardian. I leaned into Killion, enjoying his hands on my hips. They gripped me firmly as if he were willing me to say *yes, that is what I wish for as well.*

I couldn't force the words out. Maybe I needed to get out of my head. Could I be imagining that the dragon didn't want me here? Was it true the stress of everything had caught up with me, and I was simply feeling off balance? A good night's sleep and a lot of food could tip the scales in the other direction.

I ran my hands over his arms, allowing him to tug me close enough our hips touched. "You are my home."

He caught my mouth with his. Light, sensual kisses on the corners, his teeth nipping my bottom lip. My knees went weak as lust flooded my system, and I moaned as the desire that was always bubbling under my skin bloomed into an all-consuming need. I shoved him onto the bed, and he chuckled, taking me with him.

All thoughts of dragons and repulsion magic disappeared as I tugged at his clothes, undoing his tie and ripping open his shirt. Buttons flew, and he yanked the hem of my shirt up and over my head. We collapsed into a tangle of arms and legs, mouths and tongues, our lust insatiable.

"Ah *hem*," a deep voice rang out.

"What the—?" I was seated on top of Killion and pivoted around to find Death across the way, staring into the fire. My voice came out a screech. *"Don't you ever knock? Get out!"*

"I *am* sorry. I didn't realize..." He cut himself off, keeping his attention glued to the flames. "I meant to land in the outer chamber, the common area. Anyway, this is important."

Killion growled, gently shifting me aside and swinging his feet to the floor. He still wore pants, whereas I did not. I jerked the coverlet over me as he stood, fangs bared. "Like she said. Get. Out."

There was no love lost between the two, and at that moment, I suspected the master vampire was ready to shred my boss. Death couldn't be killed technically, but neither of us were above giving it our best shot.

Death heaved a dramatic sigh. "I have a lead on God 2."

He'd nicknamed the entity we believed was creating a soulless army of beings after the universal consciousness most folks called God. I personally hated the moniker and preferred Dr. Frankenstein since the jerk was mixing angel and demon mojos to create abominations. Diego, known previously as Ragriel, was one of the poor creatures the fanatic had created.

Killion's fangs disappeared. He wasn't happy, though. "Could it not wait half an hour?"

"A full hour," I quipped. "Maybe two. Or how about a few weeks? This *is* our vacation. Which is why I don't have my scythe."

"You and Diego." He shook his head. "A reaper should always have their blade and robes with them in case of emergency. You know that."

"Do you not understand the meaning of *vacation*?" I fisted the sheets. "Emergency or not, I'm overdue for a break."

Shirtless, my mate nodded. "She's right. You agreed to leave us be for our wedding ceremony and honeymoon."

"We have to go now or lose him—her—it. Whatever." Death peeked over his shoulder to see if we were decent, then turned to face us fully upon confirming we were. He met my simmering annoyance head-on. "I *am* sorry."

I doubted that. In fact, I suspected he'd chosen this exact moment to "find" this lead, whatever it was.

When I'd been the original grim, he and I shared the same bond that Killion and I did now. Since my soul had been reincarnated, it had chosen the master vampire this round, leaving Death caught in an awkward position with both of us.

However, sabotaging our relationship was as much out of spite because he detested the Undead as it was about his former connection to Grim Zero. "What *lead*?" I asked, putting him on the spot.

He didn't hesitate. "There was a life force spike in the matrix a few minutes ago. Animation magic. God 2 is trying to create another soulless being." He stepped toward the door, checking to see if Killion would follow. "We need to check it out."

"What about Madeline?" I asked." Did you take care of her ghost?"

"I'm working on it."

"And Eriling? Are you working on him, too?"

Death stopped in midstride. "You don't need to worry about him. As soon as we handle God 2, he's next on my list."

Killion picked up his shirt, an apology in his eyes. He'd agreed to take on this highly secret investigation because Death couldn't trust anyone at Soul Management Group. They were all suspects since they had the means and motive to make themselves a god. "I'll return as soon as I can."

The soulless beings we'd encountered at Halloween were only the tip of the iceberg, and yet whoever was behind this was crafty and careful—they'd eluded Death and Killion so far.

Frustrated, I nodded. I'd been the one to encourage him to take on this case. The future of the human race depended on it. If Dr. Frankenstein managed to devise a formula to keep his creations from imploding and using them to do his bidding, we were all doomed. "Go," I told him. "I'll take a nap and get some breakfast."

Seeing as how the buttons on his shirt were missing, he went to a massive armoire nearby to exchange the wrecked garment for a sweater, returning to kiss me on the forehead. "Don't get lost."

"*Baftă*," I said. Good luck.

The two of them left, and I flopped back on the mattress, staring at the tray ceiling. It was painted with a night sky filled with stars. They seemed to twinkle and dance—more magic.

After watching them for a time, I tried to sleep, only to toss and turn. Ghost sniffed about, as equally restless as I was. I got up and dressed, then took her and went exploring.

My nose for books led me to the impressive library two stories down from the tower. Ghost ran to an uphol-stered sofa in the corner, hopping onto a wool blanket draped over the arm. She settled down and fell asleep before I scanned the first shelf.

Most of the volumes were in Romanian and other Eastern Europe languages. One section held scrolls, yellowed with age. From those I could understand the titles of, there were textbooks on anatomy, history, and local legends. Also, guidebooks, journals, and ledgers.

A manual that listed different types of vampires caught my attention, and I started a collection, stacking them on a massive desk to take back upstairs.

"May I assist you?" Thana stood in the doorway, assessing me, the sleeping dog, and the stack.

"Oh, hi." I replaced a worn leather notebook with handwritten notes I couldn't decipher. I'd discovered it between two much newer fiction works as if the owner had hidden it there. "I was looking for something to read. Unfortunately, my Romanian isn't that good. My friend has to perform a spell that allows me to translate them in my head."

She blinked, seemingly confused.

"She's a witch," I explained.

"But...you're supernatural, yes?"

"My magic doesn't lend itself to foreign language proficiency."

"I see." I wasn't sure she did. A feather duster appeared and she brushed it over the desk, picking up various items to remove the layers of dust. "Would you like tea? Water? Wine?"

"Maybe some food after I'm done here." I returned to examine the spines. "How long have you worked for Killion's family?"

"This is my first assignment in the castle. When Codrin received word that the master was coming home, he sent for me. I am fluent in English."

"Codrin is the butler?"

A nod. "He has been in charge of Graven Castle since Anatoli left."

I replaced a book on the shelf. "Anatoli?"

She paused in her dusting and looked down at the floor, contrite. "You know him as Pennyworth."

I had another true name to suppress, along with Killion's. "Are you happy to be here?"

"It is an honor to serve the master."

I might have believed her if she hadn't sounded about as excited as a dead fish. "I think this will do for now." I gathered my stack. "See you later."

"I can take those to your room," she volunteered.

It would give her something to do and get her out of my hair. I handed them over, wondering if Aurora was awake and meandering like me. "Thank you. I'm going to check out other parts of the castle and find some breakfast."

"I can provide you with a tour after I deliver these. And I'll alert the cook that you'd like a meal delivered to your chambers."

"That's okay. I'd rather do a solo trip this round, and I'll just grab some cereal or toast." Or Pennyworth, since he knew what I liked.

Her brow furrowed, but she dipped a curtsy and disappeared. I called for Ghost, but she ignored me, so I left her on the couch. At least one of us could catch up on lost sleep.

ELEVEN

After my visit to the library, I pulled up the map Pennyworth had created for me on my phone and headed for the kitchen. My hunger pains had passed, but I still needed to eat. More than that, I wanted to see a familiar face and knew I would most likely find him there.

"Down the stairs, take a right, go past the great hall, and through the ballroom," I repeated several times before putting the device away and taking off.

I lingered at the entrance to the great hall, peering inside. The towering ceilings, pencil-shaped windows on each side, and two massive fireplaces that several grown men could stand upright in were exactly the way I remembered.

When I had accidentally transported here, the stone floors had been covered with dozens of wooden tables, their matching benches packed with vampire warriors. They were huge brutes that radiated malice; I was glad they no longer lived here.

The tables had been pushed aside to the outer walls, creating a wide path to the raised dais at the end of the room. Like before, two ornate thrones overlooked the expanse. Though empty now, the memory of Killion's parents on them was fresh in my mind. I could still see his mother's violet eyes and round belly, which she had protectively laid a hand on when her husband, Dragomir, had become alert at my presence.

The speed with which he'd moved from his seated position to standing right in front of me still made me shiver. He'd seemed more curious than threatened by my appearance, showing no fear in the cut of his cheekbones or set jawline.

Someone had made a half-hearted attempt to decorate. A wreath the size of Manhattan hung above a stone fireplace on the right. Pine boughs had been strung together in a garland that looped between the wall sconces. Although it was daytime, the room held a veil of magic that coated the walls and windows, keeping it thick with shadows.

The back of my neck prickled, and I turned to look behind me. The long hall was empty, the dim lighting throwing shadows on the walls and floor. The magical flames danced side to side as though a wind were blowing past them. While I felt no breeze, I sensed heavy, dark magic.

Curiosity often led me into bad situations, but I couldn't resist retracing my steps. At the end were the stairs leading up to the library. Directly across from those, another set led down. I glanced in both directions but saw nothing out of place.

Still, the presence of the dark magic made me itch. Unmoving, I imagined myself blending with the shadows, drawing on Killion's invisibility magic so I wouldn't be noticed by whatever entity was creating the sensation.

The magic faded. It seemed to be moving down the staircase. As I squinted into the darkness, my eyes adjusted to the lack of light, and I caught a shadow rounding the corner at the bottom.

My friend dread crawled up my spine, my flight instinct kicking in hard. But what could it be other than a ghost? Although I hadn't seen any yet, there had to be plenty in this place.

My brain insisted I turn back, but my feet stuck to the floor underneath them. I held my breath a moment, debating. If I'd been at full reaper speed, I might have chased after it to verify that it wouldn't hurt any of my friends. I wasn't, though, and I knew better than to chase an invisible entity when I was off my game.

If I'd learned anything from Killion, it was to suppress my natural curiosity if endangering myself or others was likely. He was a strategist who'd taught me how to fight and when to learn more about an enemy before striking.

The spot between my shoulder blades itched incessantly, and I shrugged them to knock it away. Retreating without turning my back to the seemingly bottomless stairwell, I eased across the landing and resumed the way I had come.

Two steps in, I felt the dark magic trace up my spine as if the entity were sliding icy fingers over each vertebra. The hair on my neck stood and my heart kicked hard. I whirled, sure that the evil being I'd felt before was standing behind me, ready to grab me.

I was wrong. Nothing was there. At least, nothing my senses could find. Even the chill of unnatural magic vanished. I swallowed the lump in my throat and attempted to calm my racing pulse. *It's stress. That's all.*

I purposely faced forward to prove to myself it was all my imagination. Gritting my teeth, I began climbing the steps to the next floor. Best to return to our chambers and lock myself inside until my wild imagination was under control.

Before I made it, the fiery, dark magic swept up my legs. I tried to scream but was cut off by a clamp on my throat. My body lifted off the floor and was pitched down the hallway, the wall sconces still dancing on the nonexistent breeze.

I landed on my belly, the force of impact knocking the air from my lungs. I expected to find Eriling, but my assailant was invisible.

A magical bind pinned me to the floor and choked me. My magic flared fast and fierce, slamming into it and knocking it away. Before my eyes, Killion's father became visible as he struck his head on one of the lights, shattering it.

I scrambled to my feet, backing away and holding my hands out in front of me. "You're...dead." My voice sounded scratchy and raw again. "You're Killion's,"—I corrected myself, realizing he wouldn't recognize that name—"Constantine's father."

Violence and rage oozed from him. He rose to his feet and snarled something in Romanian.

I didn't understand and shook my head. "I mean no harm."

He switched to English, surprising me. "Leave. You are not welcome here."

"I'm his fiancée. He brought me here. How is it you're alive?"

He regarded me, his aura the deepest black. His magic was a sharp-edged sword, craving my blood. "You're the ghost I saw that night."

He remembered. "Blame your family ring. It was lost, and your son asked me to retrieve it. When I touched it, it transported me here."

His black eyes narrowed. "What kind of spirit are you?"

"Not a spirit; I'm a grim reaper."

He advanced on me, seeming as corporeal as I was. "The soul eater." Another snarl tore from his lips, his fangs flashing.

As I scrambled backward, I hit the doorframe. "I eat regular food, not souls. It's a long story of how I became a grim and met Constantine. We should find him and let him know you're alive." *At least as much as a vampire can be.*

"You lie." He grabbed my shoulders, slamming me against the wooden frame hard enough to rattle my teeth. "You think you can reap me?"

I will not cower. At least, I told myself not to. Having such a gruesome, horrible, Otherworldly creature ready to snap me in two was more than intimidating.

Gritting my teeth, I shoved at his chest. He was twice my size, and even with my enhanced strength, I couldn't budge him. "I have no order to reap you, *Dragomir*. Now, back the reaper up and take your hands off me."

He reared back at the use of the name. According to Killion, no one knew his given name but those in his closest circle, and even Dragomir was a variation of it. He'd been the Dragon Heretic to outsiders, both human and supernatural.

He didn't remove his grip. "Then why are you here?"

"I told you. To marry your son."

His iron grip tightened, fingers digging painfully into my shoulders. "He would never return to this place. To me. And he would never take up with your kind."

"We're *incatusa sufletum*. Our souls are bonded."

The vampire king's fangs descended further. "Now I know you're lying. That's a myth."

I shook my head, wondering if kneeing him in the balls was an option. They were probably made of steel. "It's not. Ask him. He'll confirm it."

His face came within an inch of mine, his inky black magic as cold as the air enveloping me. "My son isn't here. I would know. Death shouldn't have sent you. You are now mine to slay."

My fiancé's dad wanted to kill me. Great. "You and I have gotten off on the wrong foot. Can we start over?"

"That night you showed up here, you meant to take his life and mine." His bared fangs were entirely too close to my neck for my liking. "Don't pretend you didn't know."

I pressed into the wood, even though my spine cried out in pain. Grim Zero opened her eyes and cocked her head, curious. "Know what?"

"That he would be born that night. That his mother was—"

Before he finished, Ghost rushed down the hall, morphing into her psychopomp form. In a flash, a hundred-plus pounds of snarling menace attacked him.

He threw up an arm, and she chomped on it. I yelled for her to stop, but at that exact moment, the vampire burst into dozens of black wings and gnashing teeth.

Bats.

They descended on her. My magic tore out of me, ignoring my mind's shock at his transformation. A wave of it slammed into the rodents with such force it flung them against the wall.

"Chloe!" Killion's voice echoed over the shrieking bats. They flew up as one, circled over us, and fled down the stairs, disappearing.

I fell on Ghost, checking her over as I stroked her fur. My fingers came away bloody from the dozens of wounds the bats had inflicted. She licked my face as I blubbered, "Oh, no. You're hurt. I'm so sorry."

Killion did something similar to me, running his hands over my arms and searching my face as he spun me toward him. "What happened? Why are you down here?"

Pennyworth, Aurora, and Andy joined us. "What in the name of the goddess was that?" Aurora asked, staring down into the depths of the darkness. "Were those *bats*?"

I nodded, legs shaking.

Killion tilted my head to the side. "Your neck. It's bruised."

I swallowed hard. "I was attacked." Again. "He tried to strangle me."

"By whom?" Pennyworth gasped, his face contorting.

"Or what?" Andy added, peeking over Aurora's shoulder.

Killion released my jaw, placing his hand on my throat. This wasn't going to be easy, telling him the truth. He believed his father was dead. All this time...

"You told me you couldn't transform into a bat and fly," I said, recalling one of our first lengthy conversations.

He frowned. "I can't."

"Can some vampires?"

His frown deepened. "A few ancients are said to have mastered shapeshifting." His head swiveled in the direction of our friends—the direction the bats had disappeared. "Bats are commonplace in old castles. I assure you, they are not Undead."

Ancient ones. I rubbed my neck, which was now healed except for a phantom pain lodged in my throat. "The bats couldn't do this," I pointed to my neck. "Do you know any ancient vampires who might be hanging around?"

His violet gaze was nearly black as it met mine. "Describe your attacker. Have you ever seen them before?"

"I..." How could I tell him his father still lived? That he was here? It wouldn't do for me to try to hide it—he would see it in my mind, regardless.

Ghost morphed into her normal size and pawed at my leg. I picked her up, cuddling her close. Her fur tickled my face as her wounds healed on their own.

"Thank you," I whispered against her velvety forehead. I lifted my gaze to my mate's. "She saved me."

His hand was firm on my arm. "Tell me who did this. One of the staff? If so, they are unwelcome here and will be dismissed immediately."

Pennyworth nodded, patting my shoulder. "We don't tolerate such behavior. They'll be properly punished and exiled from Romania."

"It was a vampire," I admitted reluctantly. "But you can't punish or exile him."

"Of course, I can," Killion argued. "No one crosses me and lives."

I shook my head. "This is a special case."

"What do you mean?" Aurora asked.

"You're always a little weird, Chloe," Andy said, "but you've been extra strange this whole trip." Aurora smacked his arm, and he flinched. "What? She has!"

I rubbed a hand over my eyes. "He's right. I'm bonkers at the moment. I'm not sure what happened."

Killion wasn't buying it. "You do know. Tell me."

I had to be honest. He'd figure it out soon enough, and I didn't want to keep things from him. "It's complicated."

"What isn't with you?" Aurora murmured.

Right. "It's complicated because my attacker is supposed to be dead."

"As in Undead?" Andy asked. "Yeah, we figured that out."

"No." I shook my head. "As in *dead* dead. He's a vampire, all right. Definitely ancient and apparently not happy about me being here."

Killion's grip tightened. "You know him?"

"Sort of."

"Who is it, Chloe?" Aurora asked. "Just spit it out."

I braced myself, hugging Ghost. "It's your dad," I said to Killion. "He's alive."

TWELVE

Everyone froze at the announcement.

Killion studied me as if I'd grown an extra head. "That's impossible." He snapped out of his shock and said to Pennyworth, "Get Moss and Katarina to check for intruders. And bats," he added. He guided me toward the ascending stairs. "Let's get you to our chambers. I'll have food and drink brought up. Perhaps a warm bath would be good?"

Pennyworth hesitated. "Could an Undead with ill intent breach the guardian's ward without us knowing it?"

"Never," Killion said, confident.

"Unless the intruder is the original owner," I grumbled.

Consternation crossed his handsome features. "Check every room, closet, and storage shed," he instructed Pennyworth. "I want proof no one is inside these walls but us."

The butler bowed and departed. I removed my arm

from Killion's grip. "This isn't a hallucination brought on by stress. It was Dragomir. He's not a ghost, either, so don't suggest it. He's alive and shapeshifted into a swarm of bats when Ghost attacked him." *And he doesn't like me any more than the castle guardian.* "He thinks I came to harvest him."

Again, each of them eyeballed me as though questioning my mental stability. Killion searched my face as he sent magic through our channel with his laser-sharp focus. I'd been under this exact scrutiny a few times since meeting him, pinned like a specimen under a microscope. "It wasn't my father," he insisted. When I started to object, he raised a hand. "I was there when he passed, Chloe. I returned his bones to this castle and secured them in the crypt below."

"I—"

He raised a hand to stop my protest and marched me toward the staircase. "Come with me. I'll show you."

I hesitated, unwilling to descend into the darkness.

With a wave of his fingers, the sconces lining the walls came to life. He entwined his fingers through mine. "You're safe."

"Your dad is buried in the basement?" Andy squeaked, peeking over my shoulder. "Isn't that where the dungeons are? You said to steer clear of them."

"It was a common practice in the old world," Aurora told him. "Many castles have underground family mausoleums."

Killion waited, patient. His thumb stroked my inner wrist. Ghost wiggled, wanting down, her nose twitching toward the opening. Fear churned in my belly—for her more than me. I doubted the vampire king would be keen to see her again, whether he was hiding there or not.

I handed the dog to Aurora. "Take her to your chambers, would you?"

The witch shook her head, refusing the dog. "If you're going to see his burial crypt, so are we."

The determination behind her green eyes told me she felt as protective of me as Ghost was. "You can't seriously want to go down there."

"No more than you do, but if Killion claims it's safe, it is."

He gave her a nod of thanks. I rolled my eyes. Witches and vampires did not become friends, yet these two had put aside their differences when it came to me. Sometimes, I wished they hadn't. "The first sign of trouble and we're out."

"Agreed," Andy said, eyes wide. "I'll watch out for Ghost. Aurora and Killion will watch out for you."

I gave what I hoped passed for a confident smile. "Okay, then." I nodded at Killion. "Lead the way."

The broad stone steps narrowed the farther down we went. With the castle built into the mountainside, the original architects had used the natural stone to chisel out each one. A sweet-sour smell, mixed with death, engulfed us, and the far-off sound of trickling water made me remember the river we'd driven across. It had to be far away, but when we reached the underground cavern, the floor was damp in places.

Killion led the way past iron-barred cells with manacles on the walls. In several, decaying clothes were strewn on the floor. I swallowed and averted my eyes, trying not to think of the souls who had died here. As if summoned by our presence, several spectral waifs, as insubstantial as mist, floated toward me. I couldn't distinguish who they'd been in life; their features were blurred. Ghost noticed them and barked. They all disappeared.

She wiggled to get down. I set her on the floor against my better judgment. "No running off," I told her.

Killion paused at an arched entrance with a solid stone door. Carved above it were odd symbols. Next to it was a display with a soldier's helmet and what appeared to be a sickle. An iron bird perched on the helmet as if about to take flight.

At least it wasn't a bat.

"What's this?" I asked, trailing my fingers along the handle of the weapon.

"A Dacian falx," he told me, pausing to study it. "A deadly fighting tool that can pierce armor and sever limbs. It was, and still is, a symbol of my family's exper-tise on the battlefield."

It looked a lot like my scythe—compact and short with a hooked blade sharpened on the inside. My fingers tingled from an electric current coming from it—magical but something more. The handle trembled at my touch, a sense of rightness coming over me. The souls harvested by it called to me, and my chest relaxed. Death for them had not been unexpected but still unwelcome. Closing my eyes, I soothed them with my magic, assuring the weapon it was time to release those it had trapped.

Time spun away, and the veil between worlds swirled around me. Without warning, I was walking on a ghostly battlefield, the falx in hand. Fog rose from the ground and thick clouds pressed down from the sky. All was gray and monochrome, and my boots were soaked crimson from the blood I'd spilled...

"*Chloe.*"

The voice came from far away. I kept walking, hungry for more blood.

Strong hands shook me by the shoulders. "Chloe! Snap out of it!"

I blinked, finding Killion staring me down.

"What... is...?" I shook the cobwebs of the vision away, inhaling the stale, musty air of the basement. "Sorry, I... I had one of those episodes."

"Episodes?" Aurora asked. "You mean psychometry? Or is it more retro cognition?"

"Not sure what that last thing is, but I think it was psychometry, only I was...Dragomir. I think." I rubbed my palm where it itched to snatch up the falx. Even my grim tattoo pinched with desire for it. "I was transported to a battlefield. Everyone was dead."

Killion grunted. "It would be wise not to touch that again."

"You think?" The irritation in my snappy comeback echoed off the stones. "Sorry," I repeated, forcing myself to stop rubbing my hand. I dropped both arms to my sides. "It's freaky when it happens."

He squeezed my shoulders without further comment, but I could sense his concern. His father had used the weapon, and like the family ring, I had an unnerving connection to Dragomir. I sensed it went deeper than my tie to his son.

The stone doorway rumbled as it slid open on its

own. Aurora, Andy, and I exchanged glances, but Killion seemed unruffled. Beyond the threshold, the room was pitch black.

I expected to feel the souls of those whose bodies lay in rest, but of course, the familiar tug was absent. Killion's ancestors had come from another dimension. Soulless by our standards.

And yet...

There *was* magic here. I didn't know how to label it, but it tripped along my spine and up my neck.

Killion's unique mix of Undead power and his dragon created a potent force. Like my magic, it wasn't entirely of this world. Yet, his energy was familiar. This—inside this tomb—was not.

He faced the darkness as if it held secrets he did not wish to learn. Maybe it did.

"You've been in here before, right?" I asked.

"A few times, but not since I buried my father's bones."

Grief is not something you ever get over. Sometimes, you make peace with it, remembering your loved ones and the joy they brought into the world. For him, joy was not in the equation when it came to his dad, and I knew he wrestled with emotions that had never been—and never would be—resolved.

"I am the last of the line of immortals who came from another realm," he said quietly, "but my father never believed I could take—or hold—the throne. My mixed heritage denied me the right, and the only way I could claim it would be through extreme violence. I was unwilling to take that route in order to fill his shoes."

"I thought you were king of the Romanian Undead," Andy said.

Killion interlaced his fingers. "My father's beliefs were inaccurate. Power can be established through ways other than violence."

We'd all witnessed his intelligence and cunning in action. I touched his arm, feeling the hard steel of his muscles—evidence of the warrior he *had* been at one time —beneath his cultured suit. He knew how and when to use force; he simply chose to do so only when necessary. "I'm glad you broke the mold and found your own way to become a leader for the Undead."

"I relinquished my active role in Romania over a century ago, leaving it in the hands of highly regarded and respected lords." He took my hand and held me close as we paused on the threshold. "I'm glad I did. Otherwise, I might not have found you."

The room, a deep rectangular space, lit up, revealing itself. The dread I'd been ignoring hit me full-on.

Run. Escape. You're going to die.

THIRTEEN

Straightening my spine, I shoved the thoughts
away, afraid Killion would hear them. He didn't
seem to notice. I cleared my throat.

"Wow." I scanned the interior, which was filled with
stone crypts, gargoyle statues, stone dragon heads carved
from the walls, and urns as tall as I was, along with some
type of bush that apparently needed no sunlight to grow.
"This is equal parts impressive and scary as Death."

He drew me inside, and the power of the magic that
resided there filled my head with pressure. My ears
popped.

At the far end, a towering dragon, carved from the
stone wall, loomed over the crypts that lined the enclo-
sure. Its scales flashed colors in the light from the wall
lamps. Golden eyes, with their center slits, watched me
with predatory menace.

"That's some work of art," I said, sticking close to
Killion.

Ghost sniffed around the bases of the stone crypts.

Aurora brushed her fingers over the top of the nearest, the massive lid carved with the features of a man in full uniform, brandishing a much larger falx. "This is the royal line of your ancestors?"

Killion pointed to an engraving above the head. "Xychel, one of the originals who came from the Undead dimension. He and his mate,"—he pointed to the next stone coffin—"Queen Hicana, were unable to return after the portal closed. They and two other pairs brought the first dragons with them and found a world of promise here. Humanity was in its infancy, and other supernaturals who had come from the stars dominated the globe."

Andy strode to the end of the room to touch one of the dragon's scales. "There were actual dragons? Wicked."

"You never told me they brought the first ones," I said.

"There are many things I have not shared with you." Sadness crossed his features and his eyes glowed softly. "My three hundred years of existence alone would take years to relate, even if I condensed it to the highlights."

He was right. I followed him down the line, gesturing to sigils that looked like numerals carved into the marble of the next crypt's lid. This one depicted another male in formal regale. "Are those the dates of his lifespan?"

"His reign." Killion strolled on, seeming to inventory each one. "According to family lore, they were truly immortal in our dimension. When they entered this world, however, one of the only ways to sustain themselves was to take the blood of humans, and here, as with all beings, they are under the thumb of Death. He rules this dimension, and no supernatural or type of magic can prevent its demise forever."

Death, King of Earth. Knowing him the way I did, that idea made me grimace.

In the beginning, he and Grim Zero had been nearly unstoppable, but she hadn't been made from the same essence he was. Supernaturals had found a way to kill her, and while I possessed necromancy and used it to reincarnate myself when necessary, there was always that lingering fact it would only work so many times. Like a cat with nine lives, it wasn't unlimited, and not even Death had any idea of what that number might be.

At least, that's what he claimed.

Killion continued, "The originals found it difficult to reproduce but did conceive over the millenniums. Their offspring discovered ways to turn certain humans into replicas of themselves. Many of the human royals of history made deals with the Undead to rise to or remain in power."

"Like Vlad the Impaler?" Andy asked.

Killion crossed his arms. "Have you ever considered the idea that the written history about him is incorrect? Think about it. He impaled his victims on stakes driven into the ground. Does that sound like a vampire or...?" He paused for effect. "A vampire *hunter*?"

The implication made all of us stop. "Wait," I said. "Vlad *wasn't* a vampire?"

"But all the lore... "Aurora started, then stopped. "Goddess be. He was one of the Vaneti?"

Killion nodded, contemplative. "Danesti is descended from him. While he carried no weapon capable of killing me, I'm sure he would have borrowed Ms. Carmilla's stake if he could have." He glanced my way, soaking me in as if to remind himself that I was okay after my death and resurrection. "Eventually, the other pairs' bloodlines thinned out, becoming the version most vampires are today, while mine remained strong. Until that is, my father fell in love with my mother."

He stopped at the end of the row under the giant dragon. His fingers touched the head of the crypt directly below it, and I sensed him drawing farther into himself.

I eased beside him, even though I feared the carving in the wall would come to life and take one of my precious lives. "That's him? Your dad?" I stared at the engraved likeness, goosebumps rising all over my body. "I know you don't want to hear it, but that's who I saw."

Killion flattened a hand on the stone and closed his eyes. His magic prickled over me, patient but tight, as he sent some of it into the resting place of his father's remains. "The bones are contained within." His tone was as controlled as his emotions. "Whoever you saw, it was *not* him."

I glanced at the high ceiling, checking for bats. The only thing there were stalactites. "You said he could shapeshift, right?"

"He preferred the form of a wolf." He removed his hand, and the magic dissipated. His voice became more normal, but I was testing his patience. "In his heart, he was wild. The woods were more home to him than civilization."

"He was a wolf shifter on top of being a vamp?" Andy's voice was incredulous. "How is that possible?"

"His shifting abilities were not the same as yours. Like all of the purebloods before him, his magic allowed for transfiguration."

"Like Aurora can do." I backed away from the dragon, keeping a wary eye on it. "But vampires hate shifters, just like they do witches. Ironic that he would choose to transfigure into an animal that vampires detest."

Andy stared at the dragon, tilting his head back to study its eyes. "We're powerful and handsome. Why wouldn't he want to be a wolf?"

It was such an Andy thing to say. I laughed, appreciating the moment of levity. "Fleas for one thing, and that awful wet dog *Eau de parfum*."

My French was worse than my Romanian, but everyone got the joke. Andy grinned. "Like you smell better, Reaper? No one likes the scent of death."

I made a show of sniffing at my armpits. "Did my deodorant fail again?"

Playing along, Killion graced us with a faint smile. "Do you need further proof, Chloe?"

Did I? *Hell, yes.* "What are you going to do? Open it and show me his bones? Even if they're here, I know what I saw. *Who* I saw."

The hard set of his jaw made my stomach flip. The teasing was over. The winter wind outside became fevered, and although we were below ground, I could hear it tearing at the walls above us. "Then it had to be his ghost."

There was no point in arguing. If there was evidence

that his father was still corporeal, I would have to find it. "Where is your mother's crypt?"

"She was human. She is not buried here."

"Why not?" I had the feeling I knew. "The dragon wouldn't allow it?"

He stared at the head constructed of bones above his father's coffin. "She is buried under the tree in the conservatory. That is what she wanted."

Ghost had sniffed the entire room and abandoned us to check out the other areas. It made me nervous for her to wander. She'd handled Dragomir, and the guardian didn't seem to dislike her, but I was overly protective of her. I edged past the crypt directly under the statue's gaze. "Who's in this? The lid is blank."

My mate's expression turned cool, detached. "That one belongs to me."

A heavy silence fell. My skin itched under my clothes. I backed away, my heart too heavy with the idea of his death.

"Upon your demise, you're to be entombed here." Aurora scanned the entire room. "To rest with your ancestors."

"I will share a secret with you." He paused, seeming to consider whether it was wise or not. Then he met my eyes, searching for something—encouragement? I wasn't sure, but I nodded. There were few I trusted more than Andy and Aurora. He cleared his throat. "This place is hidden and unknown to the outside world because the bones of the originals cannot be destroyed. They, and their pure blood progeny, possessed a unique and potent magic. The kind that tamed dragons and might thwart

Death under the right circumstances—not forever, but close to it."

Aurora's eyes widened. "Their bones are magical artifacts."

"The most powerful to ever live in this dimension." He returned to his father's crypt, brushing his fingers over the engraved words on the lid. "No one in this world can handle that kind of magic, and unleashing even a portion of it could have devastating consequences on humanity."

Andy surveyed the collection of stone coffins and visibly shuddered. "Why can't the bones be destroyed?"

"Only dragon fire is capable of it, and dragons no longer exist."

Except the one inside him. The one he constantly fought to contain. I tried to catch his eyes, but he avoided me.

"Can we get out of here now?" I rubbed my arms, cold to the bone. Unfortunately, it wasn't the kind I could relieve with a fuzzy blanket or a warm bath. All this talk of death, the lingering vision tugging at my brain... I felt as lifeless and brittle as the bone heads on the walls. I jutted my chin at the statue's slitted eyes. "That thing is giving me the creeps."

"It really is lifelike." Andy crossed the expanse to touch a scale again. It seemed to ripple under his fingers. He jerked back, brows hitting his hairline as he turned to Killion. "It's not, right?"

My fiancé grinned for real, and it made my anxiety ratchet down a notch. There was nothing better than seeing him smile. "You might call it a security system for this vault. If anyone were to find out about this place and try to raid or destroy it, the statue might indeed come to life. They will be in for a rude awakening."

"But it can't breathe fire, can it?" I asked. He shook his head, and a trickle of relief slid through me. And then, the beast's lips appeared to peel back the tiniest bit, revealing razor-sharp teeth. "And on that cheery note, I'm out of here."

An invisible force struck me two steps from the door, sending me sprawling to the ground. The back of my head smacked the floor, and I stared at the stalactites pointing down at me. Sharp, dagger-like crystals.

My healed wound contracted.

A groan echoed through the chamber, and the others shouted, but before I could gain my bearings or understand what was happening, the door of the underground mausoleum slid shut with a deafening boom.

Trapped. We were trapped.

FOURTEEN

D izziness hit as I sat up. Aurora and Andy threw themselves against the barrier, beating on it with their hands and shouting.

Killion knelt by my side. "Are you all right? Can you stand?"

I fought the nausea building in my stomach and worked my jaw, trying to relieve the pressure between my ears. "What just happened? Who shut the door?"

He helped me to my feet. "No one can open or close it besides me." He ushered me forward, calm as could be. "Move," he said to the others. "This is simply a glitch."

They shifted aside. "You can get us out, right?" Andy asked.

"Of course." He waved a hand, but nothing happened. He tried again. The door remained sealed.

"I don't understand," Aurora said. "If you're the only one who can open and close it, why isn't your magic working? Who shut us in?"

I glanced at the dragon statue. "That thing did."

The others followed my gaze. Killion shook his head. "There is no threat here," he said, but I wasn't sure if he was reassuring me or the beast. "Only I have control over this vault."

A new, ugly, and unwanted thought came to me. Maybe I didn't need to search for proof that his father walked these halls. He'd just provided it. "Or someone of your bloodline."

Killion's eyes turned dark, a red ring pulsing around the irises. Shadows gathered in the corners as if he'd summoned them. "He. Is. Not. Alive."

The certainty in his voice was laced with his master vampire magic. It resonated inside the chamber and reverberated deep in my chest.

He and I occasionally argued, but rarely did I make him angry. I held my tongue as he set his hands on the door, bowing his head. The intensity of the magic he poured into it set my teeth on edge and caused my legs to tremble. Andy and Aurora felt it, too, easing away from us to plaster themselves against the far wall.

The block of stone did not move, and my heart sank.

If his magic couldn't release us, we were screwed.

He lowered his hands. A flicker of rage burned inside him—I felt it slam down the channel between us. Not at me, at the dragon.

Aurora and Andy returned to throwing themselves at the barrier, trying to force it to slide open. Logically, they had to know that was impossible because of the weight alone, but fear is a force of nature and supersedes logic every time. I couldn't hear Ghost barking, but I imagined her on the other side going crazy to get in. I hoped her antics might draw the attention of Pennyworth or one of the others.

But what could they do?

While the three of them focused on the exit, I stared at the statue. Ironically, it seemed less alive, but I marched to stand in front of it and poked a scale. "If you're doing this, stop it. None of us intend to harm the dead or the living. Killion is your master and the true heir of this royal line. Open the door and let him out." I stomped a foot. "Now!"

Nothing happened. Andy and Aurora gaped at me while Killion's gaze was unflinching, cold, and angry. I sensed his inner beast waking, surfacing. I slammed a hand against the scale and cursed this one under my breath.

For my efforts, I received a shock that sent me flying. I ended up on the floor once more, with my breath knocked out. My own anger, hot as molten lava, had me bounce back up.

The jolt, along with my rising fear, woke Grim Zero. Like a lazy cat, she opened an eye and became aware of my surroundings and situation. She yawned, stretched, and flooded my system with raw power.

Rather than striking at the dragon again, I tunneled into the unique magic she possessed. Closing my eyes, I sent tendrils of it into the floor, through the foundation, going deeper and deeper until I connected with the mountain itself. The earth was billions of years old, and all the living and dying that had gone on during that time provided me with plenty of souls who were buried in her soil.

Killion had taught me to use my necromancy as a tool, a resource, and I'd been fine-tuning ways to connect with it over the past year. This land, these mountains, held the bones of millions—generations and generations of mortals. They called to me, beckoned me to raise them.

Bringing the dead back to life wasn't my jam, even though Grim Zero reveled in it. She reached for their graves, searching for any she could retrieve from the after-life and return them to this plane.

However, before those souls answered her call, I reined in the power, even as I siphoned the magic she embodied.

The pressure in my head grew and my tattoo flared to life. The bones in the crypts rattled, the floor trembled. When I opened my eyes, the dragon stared at me with sentient malcontent.

"Oh yeah, buddy." My voice echoed in the chamber. "Want to go head-to-head with me?" I wiggled my fingers at him. "Bring it on."

Killion was instantly at my side. "What are you doing?"

The dragon heads on the walls groaned, and dust fell from the stalactites overhead. A crack appeared at the statue's base, inching its way up a stone leg. "Give me your hand," I told him.

His fingers twined with mine, our magics braiding together. That he trusted me spoke volumes of our rela-tionship, and I had to be sure I didn't disappoint him. I had no intent of destroying the sacred space, but I also would not allow him or my friends to be interred here with his ancestors.

His power flooded my chest, lifting my hair as if I were being electrified. Unsure of whether our combined powers could force open the exit, I stood as steady as the rock embedded in the mountain, refusing to break eye contact with the dragon.

Mentally, I reached out to the one entity I knew could help. None of us had expiring contracts with Soul Management Group, and Death would not allow his most prized reaper to die in this place. *Help us! We're trapped in the castle's underground mausoleum.*

"Release the door," Killion commanded the dragon.

"We are not a threat," I added. "Not your enemies. *I* am not your enemy, and I am soul-bound to your king. I will never cause him pain nor be the one to reap him."

A deep growl issued from inside the wall—the beast was arguing.

Killion didn't raise his voice, yet his royal Undead blood intensified his command, swirling around and through me. "Obey."

The ground under our feet stopped shaking. The dragon released a puff of breath, almost like a sigh, and heat washed over us. The bones stopped rattling, and an eerie silence fell.

"Did it work?" Andy asked.

"The door isn't moving," Aurora said.

And then it did. Achingly slowly. The massive stone scraped the floor, and my fired-up limbs went weak. Grim Zero slunk back to her resting place, disappointed and irritable that she didn't get her hands on those souls. Killion's grip tightened on mine, and the corner of his mouth twitched in that smile I adored.

Andy bolted as soon as there was enough clearance, tugging Aurora behind him. My feet felt cemented to the floor, however, and Killion made no move to exit the chamber either. We stared at each other for a moment, our magics still dancing, and I felt more powerful than ever. His smile grew, and I returned it, wanting nothing more than to kiss him, ravish him, and satiate the lust that filled my body.

The door stopped moving, and someone cleared his throat. Breaking my magic-induced stare with Killion, I glanced at the opening.

Death stood with his feet planted, arms crossed on the other side. "I thought you were trapped."

I towed Killion to the exit. "We were."

"You're telling me that I dropped what I was doing—which was cleaning up another mess Diego got into—for nothing."

His self-centered temper tantrums normally set me off. After what just happened, I was more interested in getting to the private chambers upstairs and ravishing my partner. I patted his arm and grinned. "You love being needed."

He knew I was mocking him. "You're not sorry in the least."

I was relieved to be alive, and I was never coming down here again. I hustled for the stairs, searching for untainted air. "You're right, I'm not, but you should be grateful that you didn't lose all of us just now."

His gaze shifted to Killion, then back to me, inscrutable. "How did you get out?"

Killion regarded me with pride. "Chloe. The

guardian wasn't obeying my commands as it should and seemed to see Chloe as a threat. Together, we overcame it."

What he didn't say hung between us. The whole incident was more than troubling.

I paused on the landing. "Our combined magics can overcome just about anything." A comment and a warning to Death.

Killion frowned, glancing back inside. "But why didn't mine alone work?"

"Maybe you needed a boost, like an amplifier," I said, "or I convinced the dragon I'm not a threat."

"Maybe," he repeated.

"Interesting," Death said, not sounding the least bit so before he rippled and vanished.

FIFTEEN

T he next few days went by in a blur. I continued to struggle with jetlag, my sleeping and waking cycles all mixed up. I had nightmares of being trapped inside a stone crypt and more of being hunted. Sometimes, I woke up sweating and nauseous. Others, I was awakened by Killion, who reassured me that everything was okay.

It wasn't. He was brooding and quiet, a continual air of worry swirling around him. He recorded himself and me giving our statements about Carmilla's attack and somehow managed to get them to Danesti. Ghost and I investigated together but stayed above ground.

Killion and Pennyworth followed Codrin to inspect every inch of the castle, outbuildings, and grounds and discussed maintenance issues. Ghost and I played in the snow. I found comfort on the ramparts and rooflines, staring out into the thick forest surrounding us.

Thana followed me, not even trying to keep herself hidden. I suspected it was on the orders of her master.

Katarina, Moss, and even Pennyworth popped up randomly whenever I was out and about. They always had a reason, but I suspected they were also watching me.

Aurora and I enjoyed tea in the atrium in the late afternoons, and I caught her and Andy chasing each other in one of the lesser-used sections more than once.

One late afternoon, I was utterly alone for the first time since arriving. I could sense vampire magic, but none were in the tower across from our chambers.

The old, rusted door squeaked as I let myself outside, facing east and the rising sun. I felt a bit better, settling into the place and the routines. The dread was down to a low simmer, and no evidence of Dragomir's existence had been uncovered, giving me a respite. Although I had no doubt he was still hanging around, I decided if he stayed out of my way, I'd return the favor.

Snow crunched underfoot as I inhaled the crisp morning air along the low wall. Birds flew in a group over the tops of the trees, and I watched for a moment, smiling, until I noticed a creature in stark contrast to the woods behind him.

An unearthly glow outlined his muscled torso, and he pinned me with his stare. Behind him, his steed stomped its hooves, sending up clouds of freshly fallen snow.

Eriling.

I wouldn't back down from the challenge in his face, unmistakable even from such a distance. Like a magnet, that challenge tugged at me, drawing me to the railing. The rocky, snow-covered ground was three stories straight down.

My boots sent snow careening over the stones, and

my pulse raced in a ragged throb. He and I were going to meet again soon. I knew it with absolute certainty.

Never breaking eye contact, he slid an arrow from its quiver, the steel point reflecting the weak dawn light as he held it aloft, calling my attention to it. Then he brought the tip to his lips and kissed it.

My breath hitched. The implication was clear—that arrow had my name on it.

Before I could think of how to respond, he turned, slipped it back into the quiver, and mounted his horse in one easy motion. The beast spun under his goading, and they vanished into the trees.

My teeth chattered uncontrollably as I made it back inside. Down the steps I flew, not seeing the hallway or rooms I passed. When I finally stopped, I thought I might be lost, but the stone walls echoed with raised voices coming from the Great Hall.

Pennyworth emerged. "There you are. Where have you been? I've been searching all over for you."

I could barely shift gears from my racing thoughts as he and a vampire I didn't know tried to pull me into their debate over whether I needed a formal aisle to walk down for the ceremony. I found myself inside the spacious room surrounded by Thana, Codrin, the cook, and Katarina. She sat, bored, on the top of a long table, rolling her eyes at Rostina, the vampire who'd taken on the role of wedding planner.

Rostina handed me a list of items we needed to discuss, including if we were going with traditional seating for the guests.

I was still caught in Eriling's threat, wishing I'd

responded to it before he'd disappeared—at the very least with a rude gesture since we'd been too far apart for words.

"What do you think?" Pennyworth tugged at my sleeve. "Chloe? Are you listening?"

I glanced at the expanse, the enormous weight of everything bowing my shoulders. High overhead, the spirits of the past swirled in wisps, their long silent voices faint in my ears. "I need..." It came out a stutter between my chattering teeth. What *did* I need? Peace? To kill Eriling? To go home, back to a life that was weird but still one I understood?

"You're shaking," Pennyworth said with a frown. He took my arm and guided me toward the arched opening leading to the kitchen. "Let's get you some mulled wine, shall we? Or tea? Something to take the chill off. These old castles are always frigid. As vampires, it doesn't bother us, but—"

"Killion," I spit out. "I need...Killion."

His frown deepened. "Yes, of course. Marie?" he called to the cook. "Chloe needs a warm drink." To me, he said, "I'll locate the master."

My legs trembled and I wasn't sure I'd make it to the enormous kitchen, with or without the cook's help. I called him through our channel but was met with a sick emptiness as a response.

He'd shut it down while on a video call with one of his lieutenants.

With Marie's begrudging aid, I ended up in the warm kitchen and sank onto a hard wooden chair. She slid a mug of something warm and spicy under my nose. "What happened to you?" she asked in husky English. "You look like you've seen a ghost."

I gave a dry laugh. "I see them all the time. They don't rattle me."

"Drink," she ordered. "I make you a sandwich."

While food wouldn't hurt, I wasn't sure I could keep it down. I sipped and made a face at the bitter taste. "What's in this?"

She ignored me, humming as she retrieved items from the fridge and cut slices of bread from a fresh loaf. "If you're going to rule the Undead, you must toughen up."

My limbs no longer trembled, and I forced down another gulp. The second dose wasn't so bad and my throat and chest warmed. "Pep talks aren't your strong suit, are they?"

She muttered under her breath, "They will all hunt you."

I set down the cup, cheeks hot. Did she know about Eriling? "Who?"

"The others, all of them."

"The vampire hunters?"

She turned from the island. "The vampire lords in this region who wish to usurp our master, the shifter packs, the witches. You are an easy target." She pointed the tip of the knife she was using to slice cheese at me. "They will come for your head."

The memory of Eriling pointing his arrow in a similar manner turned my warmed body back to ice. I stood. "I've done nothing to any of them, and I won't be frightened off by your predictions. I'm marrying your master, and if anyone comes for me, I'll—"

"Chloe?" Killion strode into the room, his violet gaze worried. "Are you all right?"

Pennyworth entered with him. "She looks better than she did."

Anger simmered under my skin. "Can we talk somewhere private?"

He spoke to his employees. "Bring more substantial food than a sandwich to our chambers."

"Right away," Pennyworth and Marie replied in unison.

"No," I said, ignoring the crook of his brow. "I want a full dinner, prepared and ready in two hours. We will eat in the Grand Hall—everyone, including the staff. After we finish, you can ask any questions or voice any concerns about me and the fact I'm marrying your master. We can also discuss the details of the ceremony and the Christmas celebration we're going to have."

My announcement met with stunned silence. Katarina and Moss had snuck in and hung back by the doorway. They exchanged a look. Codrin slipped past them and bowed to me. "An excellent idea. Marie? Pennyworth? Let's get started on the meal."

Killion said nothing, only took me upstairs to the tower. Inside his softly lit rooms, I sank onto the sofa. My head pounded, and I held it between my hands. He seated himself next to me, and Ghost roused herself from her bed near the hearth to join us, sniffing at my boots.

"What happened?" he asked, unbuttoning his jacket. Even here in his home, he wore tailored suits and ties. I wondered if it was a show of power to his vampires or a shield to make him feel safe. "Pennyworth said you went missing again. Where were you?"

"I took a walk, that's all. Too much wedding planning."

He stroked my hair, worried a strand between his finger and thumb. "I know better."

"Can't keep anything from you." I gave a strangled chuckle. "It was Eriling. He was in the woods."

He braced an elbow on one knee. "Doing what?"

I shrugged. "Waiting for me, I think."

He jammed a hand through his hair and paced in front of the fireplace. "I'll speak to Death about dealing with him. He, nor his hunters, can enter the castle, mind you, so you have nothing to worry about, but it would be best if you stayed inside unless I'm with you."

I didn't have the energy to argue, and if I stewed about ways to trap the leader of The Wild Hunt, Killion would read my mind and know what I was planning. I begged off to take a shower, leaving him and the dog by the fireplace.

SIXTEEN

Our meal that night wasn't unpleasant, but there was a forced lightness to it. I knew the staff had plenty of questions about me and my new role as their mistress, but none were confident enough to say anything.

Pennyworth had made sure the food was a mixture of local dishes and some of my favorite American meals. Aurora and Andy joined us, as did Omwee and Rostina. Most of the conversation centered around the wedding preparations, and I appointed Marie and Rostina to oversee the Christmas party planning.

Over an afternoon meal the following day, Killion was once again moody and sullen. I did my best to pull him out of his funk, but he was too caught up in his own worries.

Exasperated, I finally demanded he tell me what was wrong. He'd blown me off every time I asked, and I was determined he wouldn't this time. "I know we have a lot on our plate between the ceremony, my family coming, and your investigation with Death, but we're getting married in seven days. You could act happier about it."

"Nothing brings me more joy than knowing you will be my bride."

Confronting him head-on was rarely a good idea, especially when both of us were irritable. I toyed with the last piece of bread on my plate, considering which problem to tackle first. "Funny, because you seem like a groom with cold feet. You're restless, crabby, and aloof."

"I could say the same of you. Are you regretting your decision to marry me?"

"Nice try. You know better than that." The dragon guardian's repelling magic was bothering me less, and I'd found no further evidence of Dragomir residing in the castle walls. Still, I had the feeling neither of those items was the cause of what was bothering Killion. "I think last night's dinner went pretty well, don't you?"

He gave a halfhearted nod and took a sip of his wine. "It did. You're acting like the mistress of the castle. I apologize for my behavior. I have much on my mind."

"What's new?"

His full lips thinned. "It's the investigation Death and I are working on."

The response came almost too fast as if he was prepared for this confrontation. "I don't believe that." He'd disappeared a couple times, discussing the case with my boss, but I knew there was more to it. "It's this castle. Ever since we arrived, you've been acting off."

"I am taking every measure to keep your family and friends safe when they arrive in two days. Along with that, there is a lot of maintenance that needs to be done. I need to restructure my staff. The regional lords have many requests. I didn't realize things here were so... messy."

I didn't doubt that any of those things were true. "Our guests will only be here for the weekend. I know you're worried about putting them in close quarters with vampires, but you and I will make sure they're protected. We've already agreed on what measures to take."

The fact that my family and friends were human and didn't know I was a reaper or that my future husband was king of the Undead had caused us each quite a bit of apprehension. I understood his concerns but also knew his vampires wanted nothing more than to please him. Outside of Marie, perhaps, they would protect me and mine to the death.

He ran a hand over his face and dropped it to the table hard enough to rattle the silverware. "It's not that."

"Then tell me what it is. We'll figure it out and handle it together. That's what we do. Remember?" I sent a replay image of our defeating the dragon in the dungeon into his mind.

Realizing I had goaded him into a confession, he sat back and gave an exasperated half-smile. "It's not their safety I'm worried about. It's yours."

Now, we were getting to the heart of the matter. "You said I have nothing to fear from Eriling or the vampire hunters as long as I'm inside these walls, right? And there have been no further attacks on me or even a single bat sighting."

"True." He fingered his unused napkin. "I've repeatedly connected with the dragon guardian. It offers no resistance to me, nor does it refuse to obey my commands. What happened in the mausoleum bothers me a great deal. However, I know that while it shouldn't feel threatened by you, I am surer than ever that it does. I have concluded that you are in danger if you remain here. I think it best we leave."

It took me a couple tries to find a response. "You want to call off the wedding?"

"Of course not. We will move to another location, preferably not in Romania. We can avoid The Wild Hunt and the Vaneti."

I thought of what Death had said to Eriling—that he was outside his domain. "I'm not sure I'm safe from The Wild Hunt whereever I go." In fact, regardless of Death's assurances that he would handle him, I knew I'd have to face down Eriling and end his hunt if I ever wanted peace.

"Death said he is looking into ways to eliminate Eriling's threat, but there are plenty more for us to deal with, and leaving here is a start."

I tried to wrap my mind around switching the location of our ceremony. This has been my dream for months, ever since he'd proposed, and things were already in motion for it to happen.

The spot under my breastbone contracted as if a hand were squeezing my heart. Moving didn't feel right. I shook my head. "We're getting married here. There has to be something I can do to mollify the guardian, and we're not running from our enemies."

"There is no dishonor in being safe," he countered. "I've made up my mind. I'll have the staff pack our bags and arrange transportation to the train station first thing tomorrow."

He was in master vampire mode, commanding and assertive. Was it worth butting heads over this? I bit my bottom lip. Everything was a chess game to him, including this. There was no app to help me with my next move, so I took a deep breath and went with my gut. "Will you grant me twenty-four hours? I want to try something." I reached across the table and laid my hand over his. "Please. For us. If I haven't resolved my relationship with the guardian by this time tomorrow, I'll do what you want."

He regarded me with a keen assessment. "Try what?"

The details were still sketchy. "I'm good with animals, and the guardian isn't all that different from a big dog. He sees you as his alpha, but until we're married, he only sees me as a grim—a threat. I may not be able to change that, but I think I can gain his trust, and once I do, he'll be *my* guardian protector, as well."

"How will you do that?"

"Just like I would with any animal—respect his boundaries, give him a treat, and show him I am his friend."

Killion's doubt was evident on his face. Surprisingly, he relented. "Twenty-four hours, and you'll stay by my side."

Feeling the fist inside me unclench, I smiled. Ghost scratched at my leg, letting me know she wanted to go outside. Her newfound love for snow and desire to play in it was cute. I got to my feet. "I need to walk Ghost, so it looks like you'll be sticking close to *me*, Master."

He acted like he hated it when I used the term, but secretly, he loved it. He drew me in for a lustful kiss before we dressed for the weather and went outside.

We trudged through thick drifts in the inner courtyard as Ghost raced ahead of us. She was light enough that she bounded over the deepest without sinking into them, and she rolled in smaller drifts, disappearing entirely at times since she was pure white to begin with. Tiny balls formed in her long hair, and she was soaked before we'd made one circuit of the grounds. Several times, when she landed in a snowbank and disappeared, Killion dug her out. She was undaunted and continued to revel in her new favorite pastime.

We passed what had once been an impressive horse stable alongside long, narrow barracks for warriors. I stopped outside a small ornate church shaped like a basilica with a gold-plated roof and a spire that reached heavenward. "Religion and the Undead. I've never quite understood why so many of you cling to Christianity in the face of knowing you cannot be redeemed."

Moss exited the church and, upon seeing us, gave a bashful wave before putting his head down and disappearing across the drifts into the main castle.

Killion chuckled. "While most supernaturals believe there is no such thing as heaven and hell, per se, any belief system offers comfort."

"Surprising that your father would allow for such weakness, to believe in anything but the power of the Undead Nation."

"It was my mother's request."

"She was religious?"

Random snowflakes began to fall from the overcast sky, landing in his midnight-black hair. They melted instantly, as if his magic were too hot for them to survive. "I don't believe she ever stepped foot in it. If anything, she worshiped her plants."

"Odd."

"Perhaps, but she was sensitive to the needs of all of those who resided here and wanted them to have a sanctuary like she did."

We continued in silence until we'd made the circuit. I was shivering, and the snow was falling harder now. Inside, I used several towels Pennyworth brought to dry the dog, and she wiggled in my grip, unwilling to be contained and shooting off to find more adventures as soon as I released her.

The butler provided me with hot cocoa and spiced wine for Killion. We took our drinks and meandered through a portion of the castle I had not yet explored. Killion showed me a few important rooms and relayed his family's history as we strolled. We ended up in a parlor with a fine art collection, from paintings to sculptures and metalwork. There was an enormous array of valuable items spanning centuries.

"Each time my father went to war, he brought something back." Killion ran his fingers over a bronze statue of a male wearing a cloak. His beard was long, his hair clipped short, and his only weapon was a knife in a sheath on his belt, yet he emanated a warrior's presence. "I don't believe he cared about the art itself; it was simply a reminder of the places he had been and the battles he'd fought. A souvenir, you might say, that had little value to him beyond marking the time period and experiences. Some immortals find it helps to have that connection."

It sounded like a lonely existence to me, and this room felt like a different kind of tool, trapping history between its walls.

I finished my drink and tugged him out of the room, continuing our walk down the hall. A balcony looked out beyond the castle walls toward the towering mountainside. Although it was snowing harder, I opened the French doors and peered over the ledge.

I shivered, and he wrapped his arms around me. The white ground below resembled cotton candy, and I could barely make out our footsteps far below as the falling snow filled them.

In the distance, the tips of the trees pointed skyward like a million arrows. Darkness would fall early again tonight, the clouds bearing down on us. The mountains disappeared in the distance, but I detected a slender path through the trees. It was narrow and became hidden when it veered to the west, but even covered in snow, the break in the tree line that created a path was clear.

The trunks resembled soldiers lined up and ready to march, and I blinked when one of those closest grew fatter at its base. Wondering if my eyes were playing tricks on me, I stared in awe as the tree appeared to give birth to a smaller version of itself; only this version had human features—eyes, elongated ears, and spindly arms and legs. Stiff hair pointed straight up, while its body was covered in feather-like leaves.

I blinked, and the strange human-tree hybrid mirrored it, its eyes disappearing beneath its thick lids.

Transfixed, I couldn't move or speak, yet my telepathy worked just fine. *What is that?*

Killion became alert. *What is what?*

The sinking sun threaded through the woods, a single, pale peach ray landing on a large stone alongside the path. I hesitated to break contact with the forest creature but glanced at it and saw a glowing symbol etched on its surface. Another creature peeked over the top. This one was horned, and the long hair that fell over pointed ears resembled fur. *There are two of them now.*

The Wild Hunt? I cannot see them.

I shook my head, bouncing my gaze between the two entities. *I think they're some kind of Fae. Not like Harmony and her father.* Those two were Fae royalty I'd met months ago, visiting their magical realm with Death and managing to save Harmony from a curse. *These are something else.*

While they seemed harmless, I knew the moment he finally noticed them because he shifted me behind him in one fluid movement. *They are Forest Fae.*

Even telepathically, his tone suggested an equal amount of surprise and caution. I peered over his shoulder, torn between insisting they couldn't hurt me from this far away and appreciating that he always looked out for my well-being. "Why are they showing themselves to us?" I whispered.

"I don't know." The admission was filled with annoyance. Killion prided himself on knowing all. He hated it when he had no explanation for something. "They haven't been seen in these parts for hundreds of years.

The legends say when one of theirs dies, they must be returned to the forest."

"Eriling was after Madeline. He said she had moss maiden blood. Is it possible they're looking for her? That maybe they can smell her on me?"

He was silent, thinking it over. Even when you washed off blood, supernaturals could detect it. "Perhaps."

"Is there any way for us to do that? Bring her body to them?"

He sighed. "The rules forbid us to interact with them."

"Which rules? The same ones you've flaunted for centuries? The ones you've found ways to work around and modernize?"

He bristled but there was nothing to it. "My concern at the moment does not include involving myself in the affairs of their kind."

I stepped from behind him, and when I did, the creatures scattered, disappearing into the invading nightfall. Once more, I felt the intense isolation of the castle perched on the mountain, the near-frozen river below winding its way like a lazy snake around the perimeter.

"Let's go back in and warm you up," he said, low and deep in my ear as he drew me close.

Gooseflesh rose on my arms, his magic skittering over me. I knew what his version of warming me up would involve, and that sounded like the exact distraction I needed to stop thinking about all of it—what was in the woods, what was in this castle that wanted to kill me, how

I was going to bring down Eriling. "I know what you're doing," I said as he nuzzled my neck.

"I certainly hope so," he teased, scooping me up and carrying me inside.

We were headed to his tower, barely able to keep our hands and lips off each other, when Pennyworth rushed up to us, agitated. As a full vampire, he did not need to breathe, but I swear he was panting. "Master, I don't know how they did it. I don't know who did it. I..."

When was the butler ever at a loss for words? Killion set me on my feet. "What happened?"

He started to say something, stopped, placed his fingers to his lips, and dropped his gaze. "Perhaps it would be better if I show you."

Ironically, he led us directly to the bedroom.

As we passed through the outer chambers and into the private quarters, I gasped. "What in the world?"

Killion's magic flared hot. He gripped my hand so hard I nearly cried out. "Who's been in here?"

Sharp claws had shredded every article of clothing I'd brought and tossed the pieces about the room, helter-skel-ter. Even the coat I had just worn for our walk had been shredded. The lining had been ripped out, and the sleeves had been torn from their sockets.

I sunk to the floor next to a collection of strips of purple velvet. "My dress." I gathered and held them to my chest. "My beautiful wedding dress."

Ghost bounded in, sliding to a stop when she noticed the devastation. She examined each hunk of material and then plopped down on a remnant of sweater as if it were a bed.

Pennyworth shook his head. "I've already called a staff meeting in the kitchen to question everyone. Would you like me to clean this up first?"

Killion's jaw was set, his eyes hard. "Leave it. We'll figure out the culprit together." He turned to me, his aura fiery red and his scowl telling me that *this* was why we were leaving. "Whoever did this will be fully disciplined. There will be no quarter given."

I had a strange feeling that I knew who'd done it, and they wouldn't be attending any meeting in the kitchen. "I'll clean it up." When he started to insist I go with him, I placed a hand on his chest. "I'll lock the door behind you, and I have Ghost with me. Whoever did this is trying to intimidate me, not kill me."

He locked eyes with me for a long moment but then conceded. He leaned over and kissed my lips. "I'll send Andy and Aurora to stay with you until I return."

I watched as he and Pennyworth walked out, ignoring the voice in my head with its repetitious warnings. *Run. You're going to die...*

SEVENTEEN

By the time Aurora arrived sans Andy but toting Omwee, I had cleaned up the scraps of fabric and located one of the books from the library, thumbing through it. I was at a loss how to work out a way to fix things.

Aurora plunked down her own stack of volumes on the reading table. "Andy went to meet with the local alpha. That's why Omwee is standing guard. He told me everything. What is going on in this place?"

I rubbed my eyes. "The guardian dragon doesn't want me here, and whoever is impersonating Killion's father doesn't either."

"So you don't think it's him now? Dragomir?" She sat across from me.

I wasn't ruling out the fact that Killion's dad was alive, but shredding my clothing seemed...juvenile. It was meant to intimidate me and upset Killion, but it was far less scary than locking us in the underground mausoleum. "It's more likely one of the staff."

"Maybe I can do a spell to reveal the culprit."

"Will it detect if there's more than one?"

She shook her head. "Individual threats require individual spells, but that's doable. I'll gather the ingredients tonight." She flipped open a book and scooted it across to me. "I dug into local fables and folklore about creatures who can shapeshift or transfigure. There's an extensive list. Unfortunately, determining which kind it is, and more importantly, how to stop it, could be tough."

I handed her the volume I'd been scanning. "And then there are the Forest Fae. Killion and I saw two in the tree line. They purposely exposed themselves, but it seemed they were trying to tell me something. The woman who was murdered on the train has ties to them. I think they want me to bring her body to the forest."

"They communicated all of that to you?"

Had they? Or was I jumping to conclusions? "Not in words. I just...felt it. Madeline is one of them, and she may not have known it, but somewhere deep in her soul, she knows her body needs to be returned to her family. Maybe they understand that I tried to help her, and they need me to finish the job." I tapped a paragraph I'd marked. "According to this, she won't be at peace until her body merges with the forest again."

Aurora scanned the page and glanced at me from under lowered brows. "You can read this?"

"Yeah, why?"

"This isn't a language I'm familiar with."

So how could I be? "Ever since you put that spell on me last year, I've been able to read all sorts of things. It comes and goes, though."

She made a noise in her throat and handed the book back to me. "Who would've written a guide about the Forest Fae in that language, and why would Dragomir have it in his library?"

Did it matter at that point? I shut it and slouched in the chair. "Killion is demanding we leave and hold the ceremony elsewhere. I don't want to fight him on this, but..." I waved a hand around at the stone walls, indicating the castle. "We're here for a reason—I can feel it."

"Leave?" She blanched. "I didn't realize he was that concerned."

"He keeps his emotions buttoned down tight, but he's extremely worried right now. About everything."

"We've all faced peril before. Why is he so quick to run this time?"

I stared at the flames as Ghost snored on the scrap of my sweater. "He's acting super alpha, hovering over me like a mother hen."

"What do you want to do, my fair damsel in distress?"

I crossed my feet at the ankles and rubbed my eyes again. "I'm not leaving. Whatever is going on here, I need to figure it out."

"I was hoping you'd say that." She shifted through her stack and pulled out a narrow volume. "This is part grimoire and part journal. Last night, I came across this section." She found a bookmark and cracked open the spine to show me drawings and notes with them. "Five hundred years ago, an unnatural alliance was created between the leader of the Undead, a pack of shifters, and a group of witches in order to drive out humans. They wanted to get rid of any other supernaturals from this region, as well. The three banded together to create a sanctuary for their kind that would withstand anyone, including Death."

"Obviously, that failed."

She flipped a page. "Each wanted to be all-powerful and control everything that went on in this area. They had to know their agreement would never work because they all desired the same ultimate power. I think Killion's father was one of them."

I sat up. "He was?"

"The fire heretic is mentioned. Wasn't that his nickname?"

"Dragon heretic."

"Same difference. Their alliance failed, but the spell that protected them from other supernaturals, the Vaneti, *and* grim reapers, may not have."

"What do you mean?"

"This book doesn't give the exact spell, only components of it, but after looking through these"—she tapped the top of her stack—"it seems the magic woven into it could resurrect any of the leaders if they were killed."

"Necromancy? So Dragomir *could* be alive."

"The spell is so powerful and so volatile, there's no telling what consequences it might have brought. A vampire is technically dead, but Dragomir was an original. A royal. He may have possessed a type of self-preservation necromancy, much like yours, that the spell activated. He could be killed and appear truly dead, yet within time, his otherworldly blood, combined with this magic, might have brought him back."

I smacked the top of the table. "I knew it. I thought I

was losing my mind or someone had transfigured into him, but it *is* him. He's walking the halls of this castle."

"Quite possibly. Are you going to try and reap him?"

I slouched again. How many brides found themselves in such a sticky situation, needing to kill off their future father-in-law? "That might be a job for a different grim. I need to check with Death and see if he can verify this before I tell Killion."

"Tell me what?" He stood in the doorway. I blinked and stammered. He waved it off. "Never mind. It doesn't matter. We leave tonight."

"Did you discover who ripped up my clothes?"

"It was none of the staff."

Which left the seemingly phantom-like presence he was determined to disregard.

"We can't leave without Andy," Aurora said. "He's with Aegenwulf."

Killion made a face. "When will he return?"

She brought out her phone. "He said it might be tomorrow morning. I'll text him, but he told me they would take his cell when he entered their territory. It's standard procedure."

In my head, I heard Killion swear. "I've already ordered the cars to meet us out front. I'll leave a message for him with Codrin. Andy will have to follow us."

She stood, slipping the phone into the pocket of her skirt. "I'm not leaving without him."

"That's your choice." He motioned at me to get moving. "The storm has worsened. We need to go now."

I rose to my feet but stayed put. "You said we could

stay until tomorrow, that I could try to appease the guardian."

"I've changed my mind. This latest attack is no more trivial than being locked in the mausoleum."

His gaze was stern, and when I didn't move, he strode forward, looming over me. Sometimes, I forgot how much bigger he was, but when he was in full master vampire mode, he could not be ignored.

I pressed a hand to his chest. "Aurora and I have uncovered interesting information about your father. Will you at least hear us out and allow me to contact Death to confirm it before we leave?"

He covered my hand with his. "It will have to wait. I made a mistake bringing you here. Once I get you somewhere safe, we'll regroup."

The channel between us was wide open, and I felt his deep fear—so unusual, it rattled me. My instincts went on high alert, and I wondered what he was keeping from me. He knew something that he wasn't sharing, and Grim Zero became aware of the new, although unknown, threat. "What's going on?" I asked quietly. "Tell me."

He lifted my fingers to his lips and kissed the tips. "Soon. Not now."

Three words, but beneath them was the request to trust him, to believe he had my best interests at heart, and that to ignore or fight him was more dangerous than he could explain.

"I don't have much to gather," I said. "I'll meet you downstairs in a few minutes."

He kissed me and left.

I turned to Aurora and lowered my voice. "I'm not

sure where we're going, but I'll stay in touch. Let me know if you find anything else."

She, Ghost, and Omwee followed me downstairs and out of the tower. In a hall, we passed a painted portrait of Killion's father, his razor-sharp gaze enough to make anyone cower. A petty part of me wanted to make a rude gesture, but I forced myself not to even glance his way.

What we found waiting for us put the plan of escape on hold. Andy, in wolf form, lay in the center of the marble floor, blood pouring from his body from multiple wounds.

Aurora shrieked, and Pennyworth and Codrin stepped back to allow her in. "What happened?" she cried.

Killion, in a wool coat, removed one of his gloves and began holding his palm over a deep laceration on Andy's flank. Katarina and Moss gathered around, looking as shocked as the rest of us. Codrin, his hands covered in Andy's blood, pointed toward the front exit. "I heard a thump, and when I opened the doors, he was lying there."

Aurora began speaking spells over him, pleading with him in between the stanzas and caressing his wet fur. Her fingers shook as she stared at his blood coating them, and tears streaked down her cheeks.

I sensed his slow heartbeat, and Killion and I exchanged a worried glance. I could smell Andy's normal scent, along with the metallic tang of his blood, but under that was the odor of other magic—old and powerful shifter magic. "Did the pack do this to him?" I was ready to declare war on them.

No one answered. They didn't know. How Andy had

made it to the castle with such severe injuries was beyond comprehension. While he usually appeared to be nothing more than a human who got by doing as little as he could, he had a backbone of steel. That backbone caused the pack in Danté's Grove to honor him, follow his leadership, and leave him alone when he requested it.

Was it enough, though, to handle the Transylvania pack?

EIGHTEEN

A high-pitched whine came from his long snout, and his lungs inflated on a ragged inhale. His heartbeat grew stronger as Killion's healing energy staunched the blood flowing out, and Aurora's spell strengthened his entire system.

Pennyworth and Codrin brought blankets and towels to clean up. The rest of us stood back, allowing Killion and Aurora to continue administering to him.

The wind roared, rattling the windows and sending a shiver down my spine. It sounded too much like a howl of a giant wolf, or maybe a dozen of them, and I moved closer to Moss, murmuring, "Is there anyone who can check to make sure he wasn't followed?"

Katarina overheard. "I'm on it."

She disappeared, and Moss followed. Andy's heavy eyelids fluttered open, and he attempted to stand but was too weak. The remaining vampires, including Killion, eased him onto his side, reassuring him.

Aurora caressed his canine face, pointed ears, and

scruff, where a deep wound was trying to heal. "Who did this to you?" she asked.

He trembled, and I thought he was trying to shift into his human form to answer, but he didn't have the capability yet.

"The infirmary is too far, and we would have to cross the central courtyard," Killion said. "Omwee, fetch bandages, antiseptic, and anything else you think might help. Quickly."

The sinister-looking vampire nodded and disappeared.

"Let's move him into the main parlor," Pennyworth suggested. "We can make him more comfortable there."

He and Killion lifted Andy, using a blanket as a makeshift carrier. Aurora sobbed behind her bloodied hands, and I put my arm around her waist. "He's going to be okay," I assured her. "He's strong."

It took an hour before he could shift, during which Omwee returned with supplies, and Aurora and Pennyworth continued to patch him up. Killion was antsy, pacing the room. He desperately wanted to get me away from there but wanted answers to Andy's attack.

The storm escalated, surging at the castle walls and continuing its animalistic howls. The fire in the hearth kept going out from the backdraft, and icy wind seeped in through doorways and windowsills. Lights flickered and danced throughout the room, shadows rising and falling around us.

Moss and Katarina returned, claiming they could see nothing outside the perimeter due to the blizzard. They couldn't confirm there were no unwelcome visitors hanging around, but it seemed doubtful, considering the extreme weather.

When Andy was finally strong enough to shift, it was a gruesome sight. His wolf body shook violently, the limbs stretching and reforming, bones cracking. It didn't fully take, leaving him in a half-human, half-wolf state. He screamed in pain, his body unable to decide whether it was an animal or a man.

Aurora was frantic. After a rest, he tried again but failed and fell into an exhausted sleep.

The nap was short-lived, and he struggled three more times, each unsuccessful. It took ten to fifteen minutes for him to recover between rounds, and his heart rate dropped dangerously low every time.

His magic, combined with Aurora and Killion's, began healing the gashes and wounds, but his skin remained raw in places. The blood running under the surface was sluggish.

At the fourth attempt, his snout punched the air and his body went rigid, teeth exposed in a snarl. His paws became hands and feet, curled in on themselves. The spasm that racked him was so fierce, he flew off the couch and landed on the floor. Each one that followed seized his body from head to toe.

Killion and Omwee attempted to hold him in place, fearing his freshly healed wounds would reopen.

I could barely watch, my only goal being to calm Aurora as best I could. His body trembled, and random tufts of fur covered his naked skin, but he was more human this time. Killion and Omwee settled him back on the couch.

His heartbeat was still erratic, and he was unresponsive when Aurora tried to get him to open his eyes. His skin was cold to the touch, and we layered him under blankets. She sat on a chair next to him, holding his hand and reciting more incantations. Eventually, he groaned and cracked open his eyes.

"Andy," she breathed with a heavy sigh, stroking his face. "We're here. You're safe."

Pennyworth ran to get water, and Killion interlaced his fingers with mine, squeezing them. We were all relieved.

Over the next half hour, he was unable to respond to even basic questions. The bit of water he drank was barely enough to wet his lips, and any movement seemed to cause him more pain.

Pennyworth brought tea and sandwiches for the rest of us. While I couldn't stomach food, I appreciated having something to keep my hands busy since it seemed there was nothing I could do for Andy.

When the clock on the mantel bonged five a.m., Killion frowned at a sleeping Andy. "Get him dressed," he said to Codrin. "We leave in twenty minutes."

Aurora whirled on him. "He's too weak. We're not going anywhere."

"Our objective has not changed." He was using his reasonable voice. "The cars are waiting, and we are leaving before sunrise."

She shot to her feet, and I intercepted her before she could get in his face. "Arguing won't help Andy," I said, "and right now, he needs to be our focus."

"Tell him that!" She pointed an accusing finger at

Killion. "You are a selfish piece of work," she spat. "A coward. Running from this place and whoever is doing all of this to us—that's a coward's way out."

The castle rumbled, the floor shaking—the dragon guardian had woken at the threat to its master.

Killion surged forward, and if I hadn't been between them and possessed heightened strength, I think the master vampire might have snapped her neck. "My concern is for the safety of *all of you*. This has nothing to do with courage and everything to do with intelligence. Do you not see what is happening?"

"Stop it, both of you," I ordered. Dread bloomed in my stomach, even as the guardian's magic broke through Killion's protective bubble around me. "You two don't care for each other, but this isn't you. This is the castle! It's pitting you against one another."

"Chloe's right." Andy tried to sit. "And so is Killion. We have to go."

Aurora rushed to him, helping him stand upright. I covered his shoulders with a blanket. She tucked it in around him, and I handed him the glass of water. He sipped before handing it back.

"It wasn't the pack," he said, voice raw. "It was an odd gang of some sort. They were waiting for me on the road from town, all dressed in black from head to toe." He lifted his eyes to meet Killion's. "They're coming for us."

Killion squatted in front of him. "Who are they?"

He swallowed hard. He dropped his gaze and stared at the floor. Aurora caressed his arm in encouragement. "The humans. Those monster hunters." His gaze came up to lock on Killion's, and this time, I saw the alpha behind his irises. "They're hunting us—a*ll* of us. The only reason they left me alive was to deliver a message."

My mate rose to his full height. He seemed to expand three times his normal size as he crossed his arms over his chest. "Go on."

"They said no matter what you do, you won't be leaving here, and that..." His throat constricted again and he snuck a glance at me.

"And that what?" I asked.

He licked his dry lips. "They intend to torture you, Chloe, and make Killion watch before they annihilate him."

Even the storm fell silent. So did the castle's guardian.

I moved to Killion's side. Internally, I battled between fear and rage. "Let them try," I said and squeezed his arm. "We aren't running."

NINETEEN

"The cell towers are down." I tossed my phone on the table with a disgusted groan. "Is there a reason you never installed a landline?"

After Killion and the others managed to get Andy to bed, we regrouped in the parlor. He stared from the single window to the outside world, body as tense as I had ever seen it.

He'd closed our channel, and I was annoyed, but we had disagreed again about whether to leave or stay. I knew he was trying to form a strategic plan for both.

Why he was keeping me from his thoughts, I couldn't be sure, but he'd been making decisions like this for hundreds of years. Alone. It was second nature for him to go over every option dozens of times, searching for weaknesses and developing ways around them.

He often claimed my brain was chaotic and distracting. Not exactly romantic, yet true. That chaos and distraction was the last thing he needed right now.

"There's one in the kitchen," he informed me, "but Pennyworth informed me the lines are down."

Moss, who'd gone outside in the storm to update the drivers, entered the room covered in snow. "The roads are impassable, Master. The train station and airport are closed."

Without communication with the outside world, I wondered how he knew all of that, but the Undead had methods of sharing information, similar to my channel with Killion. I couldn't call my family and friends to tell them to cancel their trips, and it looked like we couldn't leave Graven Castle either.

A muscle in Killion's jaw ticked, and he braced his hands on the window ledge. "What are the odds?" he said softly.

So softly, in fact, normal ears wouldn't have heard him. Moss and I exchanged a glance, our heightened auditory skills having no trouble.

"What do you mean?" I asked.

Before he answered, Aurora burst into the room carrying a large crystal ball. "This is no ordinary storm." She plunked a holder resembling a dragon's claw on the table, nestling the ball on it. Inside, a satellite view of the storm took shape. "There are three systems converging on top of us," she said.

I studied the swirling mass. This was better than a weather app. "What's abnormal about that?"

Katarina had been fiddling with a brass candlestick on the fireplace mantle. She tapped one end in her palm like a weapon. "It's magical." Her eyes were hard, her gaze filled with violence. "And we know which group of supernaturals messes with weather magic."

We all turned to Aurora. She raised both hands in a placating stance. "Weather witches are not uncommon, but they're rarer than most. It certainly wasn't *my* doing."

Killion came to the table. "Can you counteract it?"

She lowered her hands. At least they weren't trying to kill each other. "I might've been able to do something before it picked up this much momentum, but I'm afraid any magic I use now will only feed it."

Over the next several hours, we discussed options, none of which offered even decent odds of survival. Worn out, I could barely keep my eyes open. Killion took me to bed.

I fought sleep, but my system was so topsy-turvy that my body shut down regardless of my determination to stay awake and help him figure out who was doing this, as well as how to stop them. At some point, I found myself in the depths of another of my unnerving dreams. I traveled through space and time, images appearing and disappearing before I could grasp them.

I woke with a start, Killion next to me, naked and lying on his stomach with an arm across my torso. Everything came flooding back, and I sat up so fast I startled him.

"What is it?" He was instantly alert, his attention darting around, seeking the threat.

"I know how to solve the issue with the guardian. For real." I laughed with relief. Ghost roused from her bed long enough to check on us, then tucked her face under her paws. "I know why it sees me as a threat."

He ran a hand over his face, then through his hair. "All right. Let's hear it. We're not going anywhere, and we could use the guardian to ensure our safety since we're at the mercy of the storm."

I threw off the covers and poked him in the ribs. "Get dressed."

"It is not often you say that to me. Usually, it's quite the opposite."

"Har, har. I do prefer you like this." I pointed at his bare chest. "And if you want to go traipsing around the castle in your birthday suit, far be it from me to stop you, but you might be more comfortable with clothes on since we're heading to the dungeon."

"No."

"Yes. Come on."

He watched me throw on the same clothes I'd been wearing. "I already hate this plan."

"What's new? Hurry. I'll explain on the way."

The storm raged on, the beams on the ceiling groaning. Snow battered the windows. Ghost trailed along, reluctant to leave her warm bed but unwilling to miss a possible adventure.

"Psychometry shows you things about an object," I said as we descended from the tower.

Omwee had been standing sentry outside the chambers, and he followed from a respectable distance. He moved silently and blended into the darkness around us, only his steely eyes visible in the gloom.

I continued. "But I didn't simply *see* your father when I touched the ring. I was literally transported to the main hall. He and your mother saw me, too."

We descended more steps, Ghost more awake and ready to play a game. "You didn't physically transport, though." Killion waved a hand to bring the sconces ahead of us to life. They cast a sickly yellow glow on the worn stairs. "It was simply the transference of your astral body."

"That's what I thought also since you could still see me in the current time and place, but now I think it was more than that. Your parents didn't simply see me as a ghost—I appeared completely physical to them, not a projection."

We hit the landing, rounding the corner to the long hall that led to the Great Room. "Your father was curious about me, but your mother was scared."

When we arrived at the underground landing, Ghost sprinted to the mausoleum's door and barked. There were times I felt she knew me as well as anyone, including the master vampire.

"Why are we here?" he asked. "Surely, you're not going to attempt to go in there again."

That was exactly what I was going to do. "When she saw me, the first thing she did was touch her pregnant belly. She wasn't afraid for herself. She was afraid for *you*. She went into labor that night, and both of them probably blame me for your early arrival." I pointed at the door, imagining the dragon statue on the other side. "Open it and let me in."

His solemn stare was as solid as the door. "No."

I grabbed his wrist. "Trust me. I must prove to the dragon I'm not a threat to you. Please."

"What if I can't..."

"Save me?" I moved closer to look up at those violet eyes I loved. "You won't have to."

Killion flicked his gaze to our bodyguard. "I'm going in with her, and if we end up trapped, alert the others, but let them know there's nothing they can do to free us." He returned his attention to me. "We are the only ones who can."

I squeezed his hand, and his magic sent the stone barrier scraping back. Once more, the magic within the chamber hit me in full force, nearly making me stagger. The bones inside knocked together, screeching like nails on a chalkboard.

As we stood in the doorway opposite the statue, the room came to life with more lights. The dragon's eyes seemed to narrow at me, and I put on a brave face.

"Yes, I'm back." I drew Killion across the threshold. "*We're* back. I know why you're trying to repel me, that you know me because I was here before. Some part of me visited centuries ago when Constantine was still in his mother's womb. Her fear imprinted on you, and you still carry it." I stopped at the base of the carving, holding the thing's fiery gaze. "I posed no threat to him then, nor do I now. Just the opposite, in fact."

I had snagged one of my favorite blades from my luggage and stuck it in my waistband while Killion was dressing. Now, I pulled it out and held it up in the light.

"Chloe...?" Killion's magic, as well as the dragon's, snapped to attention. "What are you doing?"

At any moment, the ghastly guardian might come to

life and squash me, or breathe fire on me, or smack me with a wing. Hopefully, it wouldn't come to that.

I released my grip on Killion and held up my hand, slicing my palm. "Proving I'm no threat."

TWENTY

Blood dripped onto the ground in front of the dragon's clawed feet.

Usually, if there were any human dead, their spirits would try to piggyback onto my magic and return into their physical bodies. Since Killion's family came from another dimension and fell into the no-soul category, there were no spirits to alert.

Ghost sat near my leg, cocking her head but ready to morph. I let the blood drip, sensing Killion's rising lust for it. It was as unique as the bones that lay here.

"I am soul-bound to Constantine, son of Dragomir." I lowered my voice to him. "List the others in order for me." He did, and I repeated them all the way from the originals. "We are *incatusa sufletum*, and I will give my life to protect and save him from any threat within or without these walls, throughout time and space."

Turning to my soulmate, I lifted my bleeding hand to his mouth. I gave him a nod of encouragement.

He blinked once, and I saw the red flair in his irises.

Desire and primal need. He cupped my hand with his, bringing my palm to his lips and licking the blood from my wound.

A tangle of emotions roared through me, so fierce and violent the room spun. My knees went weak, and he clutched me to him.

I bared my neck, a sign of surrender and vulnerability in his world.

His internal dragon responded. Predatory. Its magic slammed into mine, making me tremble. Grim Zero climbed to the surface, teeth bared and nails ready to claw at it. When I didn't rein her in, she laughed inside my mind, thrilled at the power of it.

Did she realize the beast could snuff her out in a heartbeat?

No, it can't, she told me. *I'm invincible.*

Thoughts were tough to form, my entire body riding a roller coaster, pulsing with lust and our soul bond. I thought my head and heart might explode.

Grim Zero's ageless and limitless magic struck out at Killion. His beast didn't even flinch. Killion sank his fangs into my carotid artery. At this point, he was more vampire than human, and while he'd trained to resist his baser instincts, there was nothing in this situation he could control.

Nothing I could, either. I cried out at the violence of it, the pain. He held me in an iron grip, the predator unwilling to release its prey.

The agony locked up my spine and curled my toes. I had no way to defend myself.

Grim Zero realized my mistake. *You did this*, she shouted in my head. *How could you?*

Surrender, I told her. *We both have to surrender.*

Never!

Even with my eyes closed, my vision danced with stars, seeing her and the beast grappling, neither stronger than the other, nor weaker. Two very different beings who could fight for eternity with no winner.

King Kong battling Godzilla.

There was no rational thought, and I found, to my surprise, no fear. This was Killion. Beast or not, I would be bound to him for eternity. Giving him my everything felt...right.

The beast roared, muzzle turning to the sky and neck muscles straining. Not only the dragon inside Killion but the statue, as well.

The carving broke from the stone, spreading its wings. The sound of its cry shattered the gargoyles and the bone heads on the walls. Stalactites rained down around us. The magic and power exploded between me and Killion, ripping us apart.

We each hit a wall and tumbled to the floor. Breathless and dizzy, I blinked up at the ceiling, only to find the yellow-eyed monster peering down at me, its hot breath bathing my face.

This was it; I was going to die.

Told you so, Grim Zero said.

I squeezed my eyes shut, preparing to be crushed or turned to ash, but a cool breeze replaced the fiery breath. "Return to your place." Killion's voice was laced with raw power that made my bones tremble. "She passed your test. *I* passed your test."

I assumed he was speaking to the guardian, yet the words didn't make sense. I opened my eyes and saw the sculpture was once more embedded in the stone wall. The bone dragon heads were good as new, too.

I sat up in a circle of crystals, their pointed tips buried in the stone. Blood congealed on the floor and marred Killion's clothes.

Ghost bounded into my lap, trying to lick my cheek. A nail snagged my sweater, pulling a thread, and I had to untangle her. I felt like I might float away, and my fingers didn't want to work right, forcing me to take extra time to do the simple task of unhooking her.

I'd lost too much blood.

As I set her aside in preparation to stand, a familiar and unwelcome guest entered the room.

Dragomir.

"How could you bind yourself to one of them?" He stood in human form and glared at his son. "I didn't think you could disappoint me more than you already had, but this…"

"How dare you attack her." Killion's aura pulsed with vengeance. "How dare you concoct such a scheme. You lied to me." He pointed to the crypt that supposedly held the vampire's bones. "Who did I bury?"

"It wasn't me who came up with this plan." For once, the former king looked tired, worn to the bone.

"Who then?" Killion snarled. "I will end them."

Pretty sure he planned to do the same to his father.

I grabbed hold of one of his legs to pull myself up. It

was a pillar. He lifted me with ease, cradling me at his side. The room swam, and I clutched his shirt. His father and I locked gazes. In that moment, I knew the truth. "You can't."

"Tell me," he ordered.

I patted his chest, my head falling onto his shoulder. Everything fell into place. "Your mother, Killion. She set all of this in motion. She thought she needed to protect you from me."

TWENTY-ONE

The blood loss and too much conflicting magic made me too weak to continue the conversation. Before carrying me from the chamber, Killion ordered his father to meet him in the well-appointed office on the second floor.

He whisked me to the tower room and deposited me in the bed. This was becoming a habit. "I owe you an apology," he said, his voice filled with regret. "I forget that logic cannot trump magic. You were correct about my father. I should have listened."

The guardian's repelling magic had dissipated, and I felt light as a feather. "No apology necessary." I could barely keep my eyes open. "I want to hear what he has to say."

"He and I have much to discuss, and it would be better to do it privately. Rest for now. I'll return as soon as I can."

Since I could barely lift my head to adjust the pillow behind it, I didn't argue. "Leave our channel open."

He cupped my cheek with such tenderness, my breath caught in my chest. "I love you."

"And I love you. That's why I did what I did. Give me some of your blood, and I'll recover faster. You shouldn't face him alone."

He stood, smiling at me as if I were a child. "Time and rest are what you need, and while the guardian may no longer pose a threat, other forces do. Let me attend to my father first, then I will devise a plan of action to handle the others."

He kissed my forehead and left. I called after him, but Katarina stuck her head in. "Master says you're not to leave until you can walk on your own. I'll be standing guard outside the door. If you need anything, you know the call sign."

"*Accio.*" It was a summoning spell from my favorite series of books. "Thank you."

Since our friendship was typically full of snide comments, my gratitude made her brows rise. "You do need rest. Just so you know, when you're back on your feet, I'm going to kick your reaper butt."

The door shut, and she was gone.

I sank into a dreamless sleep, Ghost curled up beside me. When I finally surfaced, all was silent. It took me a minute to remember where I was and what had happened. Outside the bedroom window, an enormous amount of snow had piled up in the courtyard. My phone was on the nightstand and read two p.m.

My days and nights were turned upside down. I dressed, noticing that someone had removed the blood splatter from my clothes. Magic—there were times when it couldn't be beat. Since I had nothing else intact, it was the best I could do.

Ghost raised her head but after a pat from me, returned to her own dreams. Katarina leaned against the exterior wall. She was punching buttons on her cell with an exasperated look. "Still can't get reception." She smacked the device in her palm and did a double take when she finally glanced at my face. "Blood in a bucket, you're pale as death. He really did drain you."

"I'm starving. I need food."

"I'll have Pennyworth bring some up."

I shook my head. "I'm going to the kitchen. How is Andy?"

"He's recovering. The witch is hovering like a momma bear."

No surprise there. I headed for the stairs. "Where is Killion? Is he still with his dad?"

She caught up, twining an arm through mine to keep me steady as we descended. "They remain locked behind closed doors and the master has placed a silencing spell on the room. None of us can eavesdrop."

She said that as if it was rude of him to think that they would and even more so to keep them from it. "You're sure he's okay?"

"Define okay. Discovering his father is alive has completely upended him, even though he's trying not to show it."

"That's understandable."

"On the other hand, he seems more himself. On a scale of one to ten, I'd say he's normal."

I had to stop and blink away some dizziness. I put my free hand on the stones. "You know that doesn't make sense, right?"

"And yet you know exactly what I'm saying."

Touché. I started my descent again. "I can't reach him telepathically." It was the first thing I did when I woke—a natural instinct. "He's shut me out."

"He's pissed at his father, but like always, I have the feeling he's working this new discovery to his advantage."

My blood thrummed with the need to see him, to touch him, and I wondered how he would react if I pounded on the office door and demanded he let me in. After I ate, that's precisely what I intended to do.

We passed the atrium. A sudden urge hit me to enter. I stopped. Music, almost too soft to catch, tickled my ears. When my necromancy was first activated, I kept accidentally raising the dead—bugs, cats, squirrels. Killion had used dead plants to help me practice controlling it, insisting I reframe my perspective and view it as life-giving magic rather than something to fear or avoid.

That part of me sensed a dying orchid inside. My feet were moving toward the glass doors before my brain caught up.

"Where are you going?" Katarina asked.

Seemed obvious. "I need a minute with things that aren't dead. No offense," I added.

She planted her hands on her hips. "You're weird, you know that?"

I stopped at the entrance, glancing back at her. "You're worried about Harlow. Why?"

"What are you talking about?"

Her emotions and thoughts kept intruding on my own. Had I somehow tapped into the Undead channel? But even that connection didn't divulge their innermost thoughts, musings, and feelings to each other. "Just a guess," I lied. "You're not up to your normal witty criticisms."

She glanced away. "Like you said, it's this castle." Now who was lying? "This whole trip, I thought it would be the best vacation of my life, and it's been the worst."

"Because Harlow isn't with you."

She gave me an odd look. "This has nothing to do with her."

"You haven't been able to talk to her in days, and it's bothering you a great deal." I winked. "Do you have a crush on Killion's lieutenant?"

Her expression morphed into shock, then she tried to cover it. "Did you lose brain cells along with all that blood? She's a friend. A *good* friend." She opened the glass door and shoved me through. "Go play with your plants. I'll wait here."

I happily lost myself in not thinking about anything for a few minutes of peace. By the time I restored the orchid to full health, wondering why all the other plants were thriving while it had wasted away, Killion walked in. He seemed relieved to see me up and about. "Katarina said you haven't eaten anything. Pennyworth is bringing us a meal."

"Thank the reaper." I let him guide me to the table. Green vines wrapped the table legs, and the chair seats were covered in moss. I scanned his face as I slipped into one. "How did it go?"

"First, tell me how you feel."

"Better." It was true. I wanted him to detail his conversation with his dad, but I sensed his resistance. He was still processing it, and while it was hard to do, I needed to respect his privacy a little longer. "The storm? Is it over?"

"We're in the eye. I was able to send word to your family and friends to tell them to cancel their plans to join us. The storm has made news all over the globe, and they understand and accepted that as the reason why."

I felt both disappointment and relief. "When you say the eye of the storm, you mean like a hurricane? On land?"

"Similar. Aurora has found the nexus where the spell originated. The storm is using a trifecta of magics to propel it."

"What kind of magic?"

"Those of the alliance she told you about earlier."

A witch, a vampire, and a shifter. "Your dad's involved with this?"

"He claims the original enchantment expired long ago, and Aurora has verified it was created to last a hundred years, no more. I think one of the regional vampire lords has forged a new alliance with the head of the local coven and the shifter alphas. Although Andy's visit with Aegenwulf was uneventful, it may have been intended to look that way because Aegenwulf and his alpha female allied with the others and didn't want us to know. They want something, and they've waited until we arrived to seek it."

"Andy said the Vaneti are after you and me. Is it possible they're all working together?"

"I considered that, but that would require the Vaneti to work with supernaturals whom they claim to despise. And I find it outside of the realm of reason that any witches, vampires, or shifters would agree to assist them. The Vaneti have nothing to offer the trifecta."

"Sure they do. *Us*," I said, my voice shaky. "Grim Zero and a royal from the original Undead line. Don't you see?"

He patted my hand. "The Vaneti aren't powerful enough to storm the castle and take us prisoner. They only wish to kill us. Handing us over, with our kind of power, to their sworn enemies would not be logical—they would be increasing the likelihood that the trifecta would wipe them out. And the trifecta is more powerful than the Vaneti, so why use them to try and gain more?"

I followed his reasoning, but being in the center of a bullseye freaked me out, especially with our attackers coming from every angle. "I should reach out to Death. Ask for his help."

He shifted back in his seat. "I've made him aware of the circumstances."

"And?"

A shrug. "If we need him, which we won't, he'll come to our aid."

It was said begrudgingly. Katarina was correct about one thing—Killion was once again his usual self. He was confident that he had everything under control.

Seeing my dismay, he leaned forward once more. "No one has succeeded in their previous attempts to take your power or mine. Even if they could, the bones in the basement are far more valuable."

The bones. *Duh.* "So you don't think the trifecta is after us?"

"You seem disappointed," he teased.

Pennyworth arrived with a rolling cart filled with food. He served us with fluid grace, Ghost dancing at his feet, hoping she might luck out and catch a few crumbs.

"They could have attacked us at any point before we arrived," Killion said. "I believe they want to breach the castle."

"But the guardian won't let them, right?"

"Up until today, I would've felt confident of that. But as you've shown me, anything is possible."

"While I love being right, that is *not* reassuring."

He accepted a glass from Pennyworth, swirling the wine inside. "There are many who are loyal to me in this region. I've reached out to them and am working diligently on a plan to make sure we're all safe. I assure you, any attempts to harm us or steal the bones will fail."

"Care to share the details of your plan?"

"You're going to have to trust me the way I did you with your tactics regarding the guardian." He winked.

There was a new lightness to him. So...rare. He looked younger, maybe because of it, or due to his father's reappearance in his life.

Pennyworth slipped into the shadows to leave us in peace as we devoured our meal. Mine was a creamy vegetable pie with a flaky crust and two slices of hearty bread soaked in flavored butter. Killion indulged in a few bites of his rare steak and sipped his wine, his focus on me.

By the time we finished, the evening sun was a thin line on the horizon, and soft lights inside the atrium came to life. It was a day until Yule, and with nothing else to do during the storm, the staff had amped up their decorating. The central tree was adorned with candles that burned with harmless flames.

Pennyworth returned to clear our plates. "Master, I'm sorry to interrupt, but Sir Danesti is here. He is requesting a meeting."

"Here?" Killion asked. The previous lightness turned dark and edgy once more.

Pennyworth nodded. "At the front gate. He says it's urgent."

"About the storm?" I asked. "Or the murder on the train?"

"He wouldn't say, but he is highly agitated." Pennyworth filled a white cup with coffee and set it in front of me. "He acted worried that someone had followed him."

Killion and I exchanged a glance.

"The Vaneti?" I asked. "Isn't he, like, one of them in a way?"

With a sigh, Killion tossed his napkin on the table and got up, taking his glass with him. "My guess is the Forest Fae may be making their presence known. I won't be long," he assured me, kissing the top of my head. "Stay and enjoy dessert."

"Are you sure? Maybe I should go with you."

"I would prefer to speak to him alone."

"You said he's your enemy."

"So he is, but what is that saying about keeping your enemies closer than your friends?" He winked again.

This time it was more forced, but still a sight to see. I wanted to ask what had come over him. The conversation with his father must have gone better than I'd assumed. I touched his hand as he went past. "Be careful."

He seemed amused. "What better way to eliminate those threatening us than to invite them into a place where we control all the cards?"

"Omwee and Dragomir are on alert," Pennyworth said to him, but I had the distinct impression it was for my benefit. "They are standing guard in case you need assistance."

"Very good." Killion pulled away, smiling at me. "Everything is under control."

I started to argue, but Pennyworth unveiled a tray of pastries right under my nose, and all thoughts about the royal guard dissipated. "What is that?" I asked, pointing to a layered chocolate cake with powdered sugar sprinkled on top.

Pennyworth nodded enthusiastically. "Carpati, a treat I'm sure you'll love." He placed the plate in front of me. "Eight layers of rich chocolate ganache and sponge cake traditionally served this time of year."

I dug in and heaven exploded inside my mouth. "OMG. It's delicious."

He smiled knowingly and added several more desserts to the table before wheeling the cart out and leaving me to enjoy the cake and coffee.

I sensed Katarina was just beyond the entrance,

Killion still concerned about me. Was it good that he and his father seemed to be mending their relationship? Why did I still suspect foul play? Andy's message from the Vaneti came back to me. There was no way I would let anybody use me as a weapon against Killion. One thought led to another, all of them unnerving. A plan began to brew.

After I finished the cake, and since there wasn't a second serving, I reached for a fried donut pastry. My coffee was nearly drained, and I thought briefly that my wedding dress would not fit if I continued eating like this.

But...my gown was in tatters. So much for that.

There was no reason *not* to enjoy an extra helping before Killion returned with some dreaded news regarding Danesti's unexpected appearance.

Out of the corner of my eye, I saw movement near the courtyard. Taking my cup, I walked to the nearest window. Moss left the church across the way with a peaceful expression. I saw why—Thana was with him. He held the door for her, and she gave a shy smile as the two strolled through the snow toward the castle's entrance. They talked and laughed easily, and even though I couldn't hear the conversation, I once again knew what it involved. I swallowed and tried to clear their flirtatious words from my mind. This eavesdropping had to stop.

"His faith is unwavering," a feminine voice said.

I jerked around and dropped my cup, the porcelain shattering at my feet and spraying the last of the liquid over the stones. Standing next to me was the most beautiful and ethereal woman I'd ever seen, one with violet eyes that matched Killion's. "You're..." I stuttered and blinked. This had to be an illusion.

"Yes." She held the orchid I'd revived in her hands, caressing the now-blooming plant and smiling. "I'm Coria, Constantine's mother."

TWENTY-TWO

"Why... How are you...?" I couldn't find words.

Her violet gaze locked on mine, sharp now. "He loves you, but I cannot let you have him."

"Killion"—I corrected myself—"*Constantine* is my soulmate. He brought me here."

She was a ghost, but her chest heaved, sucking in air. Tiny beads in the intricate design of her gown twinkled gold and silver under the tree canopy. Nearby vines curled toward us—*her*. They reached for her, and the magic thrumming from the ends of her fingertips. "My son and *you*? Impossible. You're a soul eater, here to take him."

The slick heat of understanding tickled my mind. "Why are you haunting this place, Coria? You died over a century ago. It's time for you to move on to the afterlife."

She chuckled. "You think you're here for *me*?"

My palm didn't itch for my scythe. My tattoo didn't heat. I wasn't sure why, but the thought gave me pause.

She'd been human and shouldn't still be on this plane. That was my job—to send her to the other side. But why wasn't I getting hit with the directive to send her spirit on?

This had to be tangled up with Dragomir. Best not to scare her off until I figured out how. "I'm here to marry your son, that's all."

At least until I was given orders otherwise.

She straightened her spine. She feared me—feared I would force her to leave the sanctuary. A divot formed in her forehead. Her eyes flashed. They were so like Killion's that it took my breath away. "You lie, and Death has no jurisdiction over my kind, but it didn't stop him from sending Eriling. He had no right to do that."

"Eriling? He tried to harvest you?"

"Death and his consort wanted my soul. She came for Constantine, too, but Dragomir saved us."

An ugly sliver of realization jabbed me in the gut. "Death's consort?"

"You remind me of her. Your magic..." She sniffed the air close to my face. "It's unnatural. The same darkness I sensed in her is also in you."

Little did she realize how close to the truth she was. Even as she spoke, Grim Zero woke, curious if she was going to get in on the action.

The scene outside was snowy and bleak. In here, the air felt humid, the plants continuing their climb toward us. "I'm a grim, and your human spirit does fall under Death's purview."

"Human?" She laughed. "I'm not human."

Confirming my suspicions. Princess Harmony had

once mentioned that only those with Fae blood carried the gene for violet eyes. "You're a Forest Fae, aren't you? That's why Eriling wants you."

"My place is here with Dragomir. I will not allow you to take him. He protected me from all of you—the hunters, Eriling, the soul eater who came before you, but it is *my* turn now to protect him. Constantine should know better than to bring you here—" She stopped abruptly, her features morphing into incredulity before hardening with rage. "It's you. Death's consort. You think you can change your appearance and trick my son into believing your lies?"

"Sorry, what?"

"A glamour! You can change your appearance at will."

"I wish. Unfortunately, my magic isn't like yours or his." I cheered at myself. "What you see is what you get."

Her eyes narrowed. "How did you make it past the guardian? The wards? The alliance was created to keep you out!"

Ah...the truth about the original trifecta's motivation. "I will not harm your son. I have proven it to the dragon guardian."

"More lies."

Her anger spurred the plants toward me. I backed away from a particularly aggressive ivy. "I don't know how you convinced Dragomir and Constantine that you were human, but a lot makes sense now. We all need to sit and talk this out."

Coria went utterly still, not a hint of the previous fear or rage on her face. "Why do you want him so badly?"

"Constantine? I told you. I'm in love with him. He's my *incatusa sufletum*."

Her jaw dropped. "Impossible. You belong to Death." She snapped her mouth closed, once more becoming a statue. "Tell me the truth. Why did you come for my son that day?"

"What day? When you were pregnant with him?"

"I knew you to be a harbinger that day, but no." She pointed at the snow-covered courtyard. "I'm speaking of the day you came dressed in mourning clothes and trailing shadows behind you. Your magic caused those nearby to die on the spot. Dragomir's warriors fell to the ground as you brought Eriling and his riders to take me. Death oozed from you, causing the ground to tremble under your feet."

In my mind's eye, I saw the picture she painted and realized Grim Zero was the star of that show. Around three centuries ago, she must have been reincarnated and sent to deal with a significant threat. Something that would've knocked the balance of life and death out of whack.

No sense trying to explain that, though. "How is it that the King of the Undead married a Forest Fae? Isn't that considered against the natural order for both species?"

Her expression didn't change, but she paled. "My family exiled me, and he took me in."

"That's why you told everyone you were human, because you knew the vampires would kill you for being Fae."

"Vampire-human relationships are forbidden. Against the rules."

So many rules. "His nest accepted you begrudgingly because they believed you were human and mortal. They would outlive you, and you could never rule them on your own if something happened to your husband. But if you were Fae, you could undermine Dragomir and enslave them."

Her jaw tensed, and she said nothing, but she didn't have to. Even without confirmation, I knew I was right.

"Constantine was only four when you came for me. A boy. The throne was always his, I had no interest in it. He saw you and ran to your side when you held out a hand to him."

Had Killion known even then? Had he felt our bond as a child? The implication was staggering. "But I didn't harvest him, nor did I allow Eriling to take you."

"I offered myself as trade so you would leave Constantine alone, but you wouldn't take it."

Grim Zero fingered her magic, sparking it deep inside me. She itched to harvest Coria, and only the fact that neither of us could held her back. "I *did* leave him alone," I said. "He grew up and runs an empire far from here."

"You kept him alive so you could use him now to worm your way into my home. To take what is mine."

"In case you haven't noticed, you're dead. Even if you were still alive, I would have no desire to take anything that's yours. The previous grim you encountered wasn't me." *Per se.* "She was a former incarnation, and I can't be held responsible for what she did or didn't do." I told myself that daily, even though I didn't always believe it. "Your husband is still alive, and the two of you tricked Constantine. That isn't right." I opened my end of the telepathic channel with Killion. His end was closed. I tapped against it, hoping he would respond. "All that aside, we need to start over. We need to be allies, not enemies. I'm bonded to your son, and he needs to understand his heritage—*your* heritage."

She stepped closer, an ivy twining around my ankle as if to keep me in place. "He cannot know."

"Why not? Are you ashamed of being Fae?"

"Forest Fae are closer to humans than other types, and my bones rest here, where the two great loves of my life still exist in all I see." She swept an arm out, indicating the castle and grounds. "But I can never rest until my bones are returned to my home."

"The forest." That's why I'd seen the creatures out there. They wanted Coria, not Madeline. "I can make sure you are laid to rest properly."

She thought about this for several long, pregnant moments. I could see the tug-of-war going on in her eyes. "Dragomir...what will he do without me?"

"He loves you very much, and I'm sure he wants your soul to be at peace."

She stopped the encroaching vines, the one around my ankle unwinding itself and slipping away. "The plants thrive here because of my bones. The same is true for him—he thrives because of me. He cannot join me where I must go. How can I break his heart?"

"You have a soul, though, correct?"

She nodded.

"I happen to have friends in high places who deal with issues such as this all the time."

"Dragomir has no such soul. We cannot be together in the afterlife."

"No, but you can be reincarnated like me. I can pull some strings to reunite you." *I hope.* Mei Han, the head of SMG, was going to kill me. Literally.

"You would do that?"

"I'm a sucker for a good love story. Constantine reads Dragomir's poetry to me, you know. The poetry he wrote for you."

Her face brightened. "Constantine has the journals?"

I nodded. "I've never heard such romantic declarations."

A husky giggle issued from her mouth. "My mate does have a way with words."

"Will you let me do this for you? Let me speak to the head of Soul Management Group about reuniting you. Then your son and I can make sure your bones are returned to your people."

It was like a huge weight lifted from her shoulders, and they sagged. "I want to believe you. I want to say yes."

"Then do."

"You make it sound so easy. "

"I get it. Most things in life aren't. I can't make guarantees, but it's worth a try, don't you think?"

"You are different than her."

Grim Zero chuckled inside me. "I keep telling myself that. So, you'll talk to Constantine?"

"Do you believe he can find it in his heart to forgive me?"

If he'd forgiven his father for the deception he had pulled, I had no doubt this would be a cakewalk. "Under his bluster, he is a kind and generous person."

"Don't tell his father, but it's the Forest Fae blood that makes him such. I always knew he could never be as harsh as Dragomir."

"Your secret is safe with me."

She held the orchid up between us. "One of my bones is missing."

"That's why the orchid was dying."

A nod. "I don't know who took it or why, but I cannot rest until all of them are buried in the forest."

Where could it be? "Did anyone else besides Dragomir know you were Fae?"

"No, but..." Again, she swept out an arm, this time indicating the tree. "Someone may have guessed."

"Let me see what I can do."

Her face lost its hope, becoming stern. "Do not fail my son, soul eater."

"I won't," I promised. "And the name's Chloe."

TWENTY-THREE

Katarina came to attention when I flew out the door. "I need to talk to you and Moss. Right now."

"I don't know where he is."

"I do. Come with me."

She didn't like being bossed around by me, but she didn't argue. Good thing, too. I wasn't in the mood.

"About what you said earlier regarding me and Harlow." She caught up to me easily as I headed in the direction Moss and Thana had disappeared. They were either heading for the library or one of their rooms. Hers was near the kitchen, but I doubted she was taking him there. "Our relationship is platonic, but I might want it to be more. Don't say anything, okay?"

I snorted. "You're not doing a very good job of hiding your feelings, but sure."

We passed the kitchen, and I stopped in front of Thana's room. It was on the way to Moss' quarters, so I checked there first. I raised my hand to knock. "Although, either way, I wonder what she sees in you."

Katarina arched a querulous brow, searing me with her dark eyes. "That's what I wonder every day about you and Killion."

We held each other's glares briefly before grins broke across our faces. I banged on the door. "Moss, are you in there? I need to speak to you."

There was no answer, and I sensed Katarina tuning her highly sensitive hearing up a notch as she leaned closer. She shook her head. "They're not here. Why would Moss be with her?"

"Why do you think?"

She made a face. "No way."

"Why not?" I started walking again. "Does he have a significant other somewhere else? I've never even seen him hang out with any of you other than when he has to. He's lonely."

"He chooses to isolate himself from the rest of us, so don't feel sorry for him. I don't even know why the Master brought him on this trip. It's not like he needs a driver."

The library doors were shut, and I paused before I threw them open. Walking in on the two of them might embarrass all of us. Then again, why would they bypass a private room to fool around here? My logic went back and forth. Vampires were rarely discreet, and maybe the risk of getting caught turned them on. "Moss came because I requested he be part of this. He's important to me."

She had no qualms about interrupting them. She

opened the doors, stomped across the threshold, and yelled, "Moss! Are you in here?" There was no response, and she looked over her shoulder at me. "Why exactly do you need him?"

"Come on." We continued toward his quarters. "Do you know if Killion allowed Danesti to enter the castle?"

"Danesti? Why is he here?"

"I assume to follow up about what happened on the train."

"And you think he would come out in the storm for that?"

No, I didn't. We arrived at Moss'. I knocked. "Many things are happening in and around this place that don't make sense. They're all linked; I can feel it, but I don't know how or why."

I banged again. There was rustling and whispering from inside, and then, "Yeah! What do you want?"

I spoke to the wood. "It's me. I need you, and it can't wait."

After a moment, Moss cracked open the door. His dark skin gleamed under the lights, his naked chest on full display with its gold cross. "Kind of busy here, Grave Girl."

I motioned him to step outside. "I apologize for the interruption, but I need a promise from you and Katarina."

He side-eyed someone in the room—Thana, no doubt —before stepping out and closing the door behind him. He crossed his beefy arms over his chest and leaned against the wood. "Make it fast."

"Are you sleeping with the maid?" Katarina asked.

I smacked her arm. "None of our business, and this has nothing to do with your personal life. I need you two to do something for me, and it's important."

Moss gave her a rude gesture before nodding at me to go on. "What?"

"If the Vaneti, or anyone else, breaches the castle to capture me, I don't want them to be able to use me against Killion. Watching them torture me would..." Did they know about his inner dragon? I doubted it, and it wasn't my story to tell. "I want your promise that if there's any way for you to kill me, you'll do it. Don't let them take me prisoner."

The vampires exchanged an unsettled look. "You can't ask us to do that," Moss said. "We're sworn to protect you."

"These are special circumstances." I met Katarina's eyes. "I would never ask you to go against your Master's orders, but in this situation, we have to put him first. If he loses control of his emotions, the effects would be devastating for everybody. You two know about my necromancy. Most likely, even if you kill me, I'll resurrect myself within a period of time. It's not like you would be terminating me forever, just long enough to keep our enemies from using me against him. He's our priority, agreed?"

They were silent, considering my words. Moss shook his head. "I don't think I can do it."

"I can," Katarina said. There was no teasing or humor in her voice. "I don't like it, but you're right. We must place him above all else, no matter what orders he gives us. He has to survive."

I squeezed her arm. "Thank you."

"You're assuming they won't have already killed us by the time they get to you," Moss said.

Katarina rolled her eyes. "This is all hypothetical. No one is going to get in here and kill anyone. The guardian will see to our protection."

"We all know that magic can fail." I put a hand on Moss' shoulder. "In the event that it does, and you have even an inkling that I'm about to be taken alive to be tortured in front of him, do what you have to do to take that option away. This fail-safe isn't perfect, but if you have the chance, I want you to use it."

Moss blew out an audible breath. "Fine."

"Promise me."

He rubbed his cross and rolled his eyes. "I promise."

I pinned Katarina with a look. She threw up her hands. "I already said I'd do it."

"Give me your word. Swear to it."

"I swear." Anger flashed in her eyes. "I'll even enjoy it, Reaper."

I pinched her bicep. "There's the enforcer I'm looking for. Now, let's go see Killion, but you two keep this our secret, okay?"

They nodded, and Moss retrieved his shirt. Thana exited the room with him. "I don't understand," her dark-eyed gaze bounced between the three of us. "Am I in trouble? Is there something you need, Mistress?"

"You're not in trouble," I told her. "I just need Moss for a few minutes."

Her lips tightened, and I could see she held back her

aggravation. He kissed her cheek. "I'll make it up to you," he said.

That made her smile, and she nodded before hurrying off.

"You owe me." Moss fell into step beside me. "The first time in ages I've clicked with someone, and you have to interrupt at a crucial moment."

"I saw the two of you come out of the church. Is she Catholic, too?"

Although he was a vampire, and they tended to be light on their feet, his pounded the stones under us, echoing slightly in the hallway. "Jewish, what does that matter?"

"It doesn't, I was just curious."

"If we're still here for the Christmas celebration, don't be surprised if she doesn't come."

"We can certainly add something to honor her beliefs."

"You'd do that?"

I thought about Coria. "All faiths are welcome for any holiday celebration."

He gave me a satisfied smile. "Why are we going to see the Master?"

I explained about Danesti. "I want to know what's going on, and if Killion's allowed the royal guard inside, I want to be sure your master is safe."

"You underestimate him, you know that?" Katarina said. "He knows what he's doing."

They all underestimated me on a regular basis. I hated it. "I worry, okay? Shoot me. I'm following a hunch."

All three of us could sense him as we approached the first-floor study. Voices came from inside, and I gave my companions a pointed glance when none of us recognized them. "Where are Omwee and Dragomir?" I whispered.

Both shook their heads, their rising concern skittering over my skin. "You do have good hunches sometimes," Katarina whispered back.

I threw open the doors, marching inside with them on my heels, only to stop short. Danesti was present and had brought others. From the magics radiating off of them, we now had guests that included a very old male vampire, a female shifter, and a male witch.

Behind his massive desk, Killion smiled like the cat who'd trapped the canary and was about to pounce. Our channel opened, and I heard him clearly—*perfect timing*.

I glanced at each of those gathered, my stomach twisting in knots. *Keeping your friends close or your enemies closer?*

Both. He stood and gestured to me. "Friends, I'd like to introduce my bride. This is Chloe Frost, and she's about to become queen of the Romanian Undead."

TWENTY-FOUR

This was where I was supposed to say, "Hello, nice to meet you." However, I wasn't feeling gracious.

I studied each of our guests, ending with Danesti. "I didn't think I'd see you again. It must be important for you to come out in this storm."

He shifted uncomfortably on a high-backed chair in the corner. The unknown vampire idled at the fireplace, an elbow resting on the mantle as he scanned me. The shifter female prowled along the built-in bookcase, trailing her fingers over the spines. She barely glanced my way, but her nose twitched. She was sniffing me.

The witch, perched on the sofa's edge, came to his feet, throwing his arms wide. "Chloe, we've heard so much about you." He grabbed one of my hands between his, and prickly magic zapped my palm. It spread like a lace glove over my fingers and wrist. "I'm Ulric. You are cute as a bug. Everything we've heard about how you took on the *strigoi* in America led me to believe you'd be... scarier."

Probing my magic and taunting me in the first thirty seconds? So impolite. He had a thick ward around his thoughts, but there was a crack, like a peephole. Through it, I saw myself alone and naked, racing through the forest, a pack of creatures on my trail.

Whether he did that intentionally or not, I'd played enough games with various members of the supernatural community to suppress my urge to strangle him. I removed my hand from his clasp, shaking it to fling off his greasy, prickly magic. "Have you heard the saying don't judge a book by its cover?" I grinned and shoved a thought back at him—me dragging his naked body over a bed of cut glass.

He sucked in a breath and straightened. "Rude," he muttered under his breath.

Message received. My grin widened.

Killion gave introductions. "Chloe, Ulric is the head witch in this region." He gestured to the prowling female. "Asteria leads the local shifter pack with Aegenwulf, and Lord Morag"—he turned to the vampire whose dark gaze bored into mine—"handles this area when I'm gone."

The guardian had allowed all four to enter, so they weren't a threat. Yet, my internal warning system was blaring loudly. In my head, Killion encouraged me to welcome them. *Play along.*

Danesti remained quiet and calm, yet underneath his bland expression, I sensed he was as on edge as I was. "Excuse my interruption," I said without a hint of apology in my tone. "I wanted to speak to Killion and didn't realize he was entertaining."

Asteria stopped prowling. "We intended to call sooner and extend our congratulations but decided it would be wise to allow you to get your bearings before we barged in."

Killion strolled to the bar cart and poured brandy into a snifter. With a simple glance, he inquired of the rest if they wanted a drink. All shook their heads, and then he glanced my way.

Alcohol was the last thing I wanted. I mimicked the others with the head shake, mentally urging him to make an excuse so I could speak to him.

He recapped the crystal goblet before returning to his desk and resuming his seat. Calm, relaxed, and completely in charge. Also, completely ignoring my mental plea for a private discussion. He set down the amber-colored liquid without drinking and eased back in the chair. "As I was telling them," he said to me, "we appreciate their acceptance of our bond, and I have invited them to the ceremony."

Me: *You didn't.*

Killion: *Trust me, they must attend.*

Lord Morag removed his elbow from the mantle and clasped his hands in front of him. He wore an elaborate velvet dinner coat over black dress pants. His slicked-back hair was sprinkled with white, and he sported a thick but well-trimmed mustache. The overall effect made him look like he'd just stepped out of a Vincent Price movie. "The Undead Nation is honored to have a grim reaper join our ranks. There will be many gifts arriving shortly from all the regional lords, as well as our underlings."

"How...wonderful," I responded, my tone lacking enthusiasm. I had the strongest urge to find a stake.

"We can't lug a bunch of gifts back to America," Katarina said. "Tell them to check the bridal registry at Harrods. That's how we do it in the modern world."

She was tapping on her phone. I lowered my voice. "We're not registered at Harrods."

She glanced up, grinning. "You are now."

Killion cleared his throat. "Our friends have insight into the storm."

Me: *Do you trust them?*

Killion: *No, but I want them to show their hand.*

Me: *We outnumber them, but they each have a lot of power.*

Killion: *We hold more by keeping them within these walls.*

I stalked the room, itchy and wishing I had my scythe. I ventured close enough to each so I could probe their magic. I didn't try to hide it, and they didn't seem surprised. This was my house, even if Killion and I weren't married yet, and I had the right to know who I was dealing with. "Aurora said the storm is magical." I pinned Ulric with a stare. My awareness buzzed with the approach of the witch and Andy. Good. She must have felt my anxiety and was coming to shore up the battlements. "What do you know about it?"

His black eyeliner crinkled when he smiled. "I heard your best friend is one of us. You have good taste." He peeked around the hulking Moss and out the open doors as if she might be near. He probably felt her approaching. "I hope I get to meet her."

Careful what you wish for.

She burst into the room in a swirl of red chiffon and blistering magic. Andy followed. She sidled up to me and threw an arm around my shoulder. "She has excellent taste." Her magic engulfed me, a barrier to Ulric's. "Keep your hands off her."

A cunning look crossed his narrow face. "Well, aren't you a saucy one?"

Andy planted himself on Aurora's other side, the three of us forming a wall. Moss and Katarina stood directly behind us. "You don't know the half of it," Andy lipped off.

Aurora elbowed him in the ribs, causing him to grunt, but he grinned like a wolf in love. Asteria watched it all with curiosity. "What's your involvement with the storm?" Aurora demanded of the male witch.

Ulric placed a hand over his heart, looking hurt that she would suggest such a thing. "I'm trying to help strangle it."

She didn't believe him, and neither did I. Before I could state that fact, he reached out and grabbed my hand. "I swear to you, I'm searching for answers, just like you."

Prickly thorns of magic pierced my skin. I hit him full force with a slap of magic that sent him flying. He collided with a credenza and crumpled to the floor in a heap. "Touch me again, and I'll make good on my earlier promise."

The others tensed, looking confused about my

unspoken promise. Katarina snickered. "Witches gonna need stitches," she sing-songed under her breath.

Killion cleared his throat. Beneath his carefully controlled expression, I felt his rage at Ulric mix with his disappointment with my outburst. "Do not come into my home and test my fiancée," he warned all of them. "You will regret it."

Ulric spluttered, rubbing the back of his head. "You haven't lived in this territory since I became head of the coven. Your kind and mine don't mix. It's my responsibility to gather as much information as possible about both of you to protect my family. You would do the same in my shoes."

He'd gotten a dose of my magic, which was probably what he wanted all along, but his excuse made sense. "Pre-wedding stress," I said by way of an apology that wasn't truly one. I offered him a hand, my magic ready to give him another dose. "I'm a little testy right now."

He shot me a glare and refused my help, standing on his own and adjusting his clothing.

"Of course. Totally understandable, my dear," Lord Morag said. "And here we are, having crashed your party and invited ourselves in at this inopportune time. We do apologize."

A wave of dizziness hit me out of the blue. Even though I felt better, my body had not entirely recovered from the previous night's activities and the shock of seeing Coria. I sat on the far end of the sofa, and while he didn't physically move, Danesti seemed to draw away from me. I guess I couldn't blame him. It wasn't every day a reaper sat by you.

Asteria seemed bored, picking at her nails. "The second wave of the storm will be on us any minute. Can we speed this up?"

At least she was no longer pretending this was a friendly visit.

Danesti eased forward, placing his elbows on his knees. "The original pact between Killion's father and the others was meant to last a hundred years. It's been over five, but the spell is disintegrating and has for some time. It's causing all kinds of issues, the least of which is this storm."

So he knew the details. Interesting.

Morag fiddled with his cufflinks. "It appears it is empowering your reaper friend," he said to me. "The Wild Hunt has descended upon all of us. I've lost three of my nest this week alone."

Asteria bit a nail, keeping a close eye on Andy. "We've also lost two important members of our pack."

Ulric brushed imaginary dirt from his pants. "My coven has been hit the hardest. We've lost five, all at the tip of Eriling's arrows."

Grief and fear leaked from their auras. I understood why. "He's no friend of mine," I said.

"But he is," Ulric argued. "Or he was. Back in the day when you were in charge?"

He knew about Grim Zero? "Death has always been in charge of reapers." I rubbed my temple, wishing my energy would reboot itself. I glanced at Killion. "What can we do to destroy the spell and its effects?"

"Create a new one," Ulric and Aurora answered at the same time.

They glanced at each other. He looked intrigued; she looked annoyed.

I sank down into the comfortable cushions. "I don't see how the deteriorating one could be strengthening Eriling. He can't harvest souls whose contracts aren't expired without getting into trouble with Soul Management Group, and from what I understand, he only has dominion over the Forest Fae and their progeny."

Killion's magic tried to prop me up, but I was far too comfortable, my eyelids beginning to feel heavy. Was this really an aftereffect of losing so much blood last night? Or had Ulric's prickly magic done something to me?

"It seems he regularly oversteps his boundaries," Killion informed the group. Death must have told him that much. "Regardless, the spell is as out of control as he is, fueling his desire to wipe out supernaturals in this territory."

I turned my focus to the two witches. "If we create a new pact with a new spell, will it stop him?"

Asteria dropped her hand and practically snarled. "We're not making an agreement with you. For all we know, you're in league with Eriling. This pact is between vampires, shifters, and witches."

Andy put up placating hands. "Chloe is on our side. If anyone can bring The Wild Hunt to heal, I'm placing bets on her."

His confidence in me was better at reviving my energy than a shot of espresso. I forced my spine to straighten and sat taller. A gust of wind hit the windows, rattling them. "If the broken spell is backfiring and giving Eriling power, you need to get the new spell up and working fast. You're the experts at this, but throwing a little grim magic at it might boost your odds of shutting him down."

Lord Morag stroked his mustache. "An interesting idea."

Aurora motioned at Ulric. "We need to research. Follow me."

They passed Moss and Katarina on their way out. I wanted to shout at her to be careful. To send Moss and Katarina with them. I did neither; Death appeared right in front of me, making me jump and hit the back of the sofa hard enough that it rocked. "You. Outside."

"We're kind of in the middle of something," I said to him, and then I realized he was only showing himself to me. Killion arched a brow while the others frowned. Reluctantly, I sent a mental message to him and headed for the door. "I'll be back in a minute," I stated verbally.

"Want me to come?" Moss muttered as I passed him.

"Stay with your Master," I insisted.

I closed the doors behind me before I turned to find my boss loitering against a large marble table with an antique vase overflowing with flowers that were nowhere near in season. He plucked an aster from it and began tearing off the petals. They dropped one by one to the floor at his feet. "Why would you do that?"

"Do what? Offer to help them with their spell?"

He glared in answer.

"Eriling is out of control, and somebody needs to stop him. If you and SMG won't do it, I will."

"You let him drain you to near death." His words

came out soft, shocked. "Tell me you haven't ingested any of his blood since it happened."

I reared back, the right turn he'd taken making me blink in confusion. "Wait. You're upset over what I did last night?" More glaring. I sighed. "Don't worry. I asked, but he wouldn't give me any." I stared at his ashen face. "I needed to prove to the castle's guardian that I wasn't a threat. That's why I did it."

"Promise me you won't drink his blood for the next seventy-two hours."

The ramifications registered, and I felt my already shaky legs tremble. How could I have forgotten? "You know it takes more than one draining and exchange for a vampire to turn someone. Even if I did drink his blood, I wouldn't become Undead."

"You're not like humans or other supernaturals. One time could be enough, and with your abilities, there's no telling what kind of monster the blending of your powers could create."

A new wave of shock hit, along with irritation. He wasn't worried about my well-being. He was scared I'd become something he couldn't control. "Well, we don't want that, do we?"

The flower was shredded. He started on a second. "Promise me. Seventy-two hours."

While I occasionally took Killion's blood during intimate moments, I had no desire to become a vampire or any kind of monster that needed it to survive. "Relax. I won't, okay?"

Like I'd done earlier with Moss and Katarina, he pressed. "I want your word."

"Fine. I promise."

His relief was evident. "The reason Smudgie has found Eriling challenging to control is due to that bloody spell, and the biggest reason it's backfired is because—"

The second half of the storm hit with a massive roll of thunder that shook the castle.

The lights went out, and we were plunged into darkness.

TWENTY-FIVE

Shouts rang out on the other side of the doors, then I heard a crash. Blind, I lunged in the general direction of the entrance, grabbing at the handles. They did not give.

The storm went into full rage mode, slamming the castle like a hundred dragons seizing it. I was blind, and my lack of vision unnerved me, but the noises coming from outside, as well as behind the doors, chilled me to the bone.

"Killion!" I beat on the wood panels. "I can't get in!"

Someone howled—Andy or Asteria? I turned in the general direction where Death had been. "Do something! Give us some light!"

"Chloe, I—" his voice cut off with a keen, deep grunt, and then all I heard was a gurgling noise.

"Death?" I stepped toward him in the complete darkness, hands outstretched. "What's wrong?" A solid weight tipped into me, taking me to the floor.

The impact knocked the air from my lungs. He

outweighed me by at least a hundred pounds. "Get off," I gasped, shoving at his shoulders.

He didn't respond, and I couldn't for the life of me push him off. His entire linebacker frame covered me, as suffocating as the complete and utter darkness.

My hand hit something protruding from his back. Everything in me stilled. While it wasn't made of wood, a shudder ran through me from the visceral memory of the stake that had been shoved into my own back. The magic coming from it was raw and powerful.

Otherworldly.

The temperature in the room dropped. I screamed Killion's name down our connection, desperate for any sign he was okay. My normal strength was too depleted, and I reached inside to yank Grim Zero front and center. She didn't appreciate the treatment and roared to the surface, slamming into my mind.

My crown felt like it would explode, but it was enough to power me up and roll Death sideways. I did my best not to let him land wrong and drive the stake deeper, then scrambled to my hands and knees to grip the protruding end.

There was no answer from Killion, and my hands shook. "Death," I ordered. "Wake up and help me."

I yanked hard, but it didn't budge. The storm's fury shook the floor beneath me. All sound from inside the library had gone silent, and I debated between scrambling to the doors again and trying to find a way in or staying with Death and working to revive him.

"You *can't* die." Words tumbled from my mouth, half of them making no sense. I yanked and tugged and whimpered when my strength ebbed. My ears buzzed, and my head throbbed. I searched frantically for Grim Zero, but she seemed immobile, shocked at the realization that the entity she'd been created to protect and with whom she shared a soul bond appeared to be dead. "Snap out of it," I snarled at her. "Help me!"

She jolted as if I'd slapped her across the face, and a new wave of power flowed through me. My hands glowed with it and shed illumination on Death.

"Well, that's new," I muttered to myself. I illuminated my boss and felt my stomach churn.

The stake was carved from bone.

The magic imprint felt like...dragon.

A stake created from dragon bone? Reapers keepers, how had someone gotten hold of that? I glanced around the hall. More importantly, where were they now?

I placed a hand on Death's chest, and the other gripped the stake with my newfound strength. I jerked, cursing under my breath, but it resisted all of my efforts.

Killion's magic trickled through our bond, his voice staticky. *Are you...all...right?*

Me, swamped with relief: *I'm fine, but Death isn't. What's going on in there?*

Killion: *Our enemies have banded together to overthrow me.*

Me: *How did they get in if the guardian—*

Something pricked my neck, and searing heat zapped down my shoulder and into my chest. My limbs locked up, and my telepathy shut down. Paralyzed, I tumbled sideways, falling next to Death.

Grim Zero's power ebbed, and the glow in my hands

disappeared, but the room was illuminated with an unnatural light. Three people came into view— Eriling, Ulric, and the vampire hunter from the train—Carmilla. She held a syringe, her face lit with a manic joy.

Ulric kicked me in the side. "Look who's been stripped of her power."

Eriling shoved him away, grabbing me by the front of my shirt and lifting my upper body off the ground. Grim Zero surged inside me, but my limbs were unable to respond. United, we stared into his eyes.

"We are together again," he said, his silver hair curling around his shoulders. "It seems this is a good night for hunting."

Ulric crossed his arms. "Your shifter friend was instrumental in helping us neutralize the guardian's power. Of course, it was my expertise that figured out a way to do it."

Thana came running up. "I was the one who gave you the key." She withdrew a necklace from under her collar, a splinter of a skeletal finger.

Dragon bone.

How did she get that? She would have had to enter the crypt.

Eriling yelled toward the doors. "Bring him!"

They flew open, but I couldn't see inside due to the angle at which he held me. The magic that poured out of the room smelled like pepper and made me want to sneeze.

He dragged me down the hall, and I did my best to see who was following. I had no idea what had happened to Aurora, Andy, Moss, or Katarina. The only thing I did realize was that Killion was being dragged behind me by Morag and someone else. He was as paralyzed as I was.

My mate. Talk to me.

There was no reply. Was he dead? Unconscious?

Eriling hauled me down the steps and to the dungeon, the stones a battering ram to my body. He tossed me against the wall like a sack of potatoes, and I landed in a half-sitting position near the entrance to the mausoleum. Across the way, Marie and Codrin lay dead.

Thana, Morag, Ulric, and Carmilla followed, blocking my vision as they crowded around in the area in front of the underground crypt. I didn't see Danesti.

My blood called to Killion's as Asteria dragged him forward. In my head, I screamed for him to wake up, to assure me he was alive, but there was no response, inwardly or outwardly.

She dropped him at Eriling's feet, and there was so much pent-up rage inside of me, so much pressure in my throat that needed to get out, that a sound erupted from my lips. Not words, but an eerie, keening noise that echoed off the walls. All eyes snapped to me, incredulous.

The leader of The Wild Hunt kneeled before me, scanning my face. "The drug must be wearing off faster than I anticipated." He drew a finger down my cheek, pinched my chin between his thumb and finger, and lifted my face. "Bring me his blood."

Ulric removed an athame from his belt and, without mercy, sliced open Killion's neck.

TWENTY-SIX

The outrage inside me burst free. "*No!*"

My hand clamped around Eriling's wrist. He smacked me across the cheek hard enough to snap my head sideways. My legs wouldn't work, and my grip loosened enough that he jerked free from it. In a reverse move, he latched onto my wrist and held out my palm. "Pour some of the blood here."

Ulric was collecting it in a container and stopped long enough to dribble some on my palm. Morag inhaled as if the scent were heavenly.

Eriling rubbed it on all my fingers, and the magic seared my skin, clearing my vision and causing the pain in my cheek to recede. "What...are you doing?" I muttered.

He studied me, a specimen he didn't quite understand. A nuisance who would not behave. "You are a hell cat, aren't you?"

"I...will...kill you," I ground out.

He turned me, raising me so my back was to his chest.

Taking my bloodied hand, he placed it on the stone next to the door. "You are bonded to the vampire. I smell it on you. Combined with his blood, you will give me what I want."

"What *we* want," Carmilla corrected.

I tried to pull away, but it was as if the stones reached out to suck in the blood, feeding on the magic and my direct link to Killion. The guardian was awake, and I couldn't fathom why it hadn't attacked the group, but I sensed Killion's inner beast stir.

That was good, right? If his inner dragon was still alive, that meant he was. *Fight,* I ordered him. *You're a hybrid with limitless power. Use it!*

Being connected now to that beast was a heady cocktail. Grim Zero inhaled, breathing in the otherworldly magic, and supernovas burst behind my eyelids. My body spasmed, back arching.

Eriling pressed my palm harder against the stone. "Open the door."

The barrier shimmered under my touch, his words echoing inside my head. Resisting, I gritted my teeth, clamping down hard on the flowing magic. *Don't do it,* I commanded the guardian.

"Bring me the blood," Eriling snapped his fingers, and Ulric handed him the receptacle. He placed the rim to my lips, and the heady scent of Killion's blood filled my nose, rich and fragrant. "Drink."

Grim Zero urged me to do it. *The blood will heal you and strengthen me.*

But Death's warning rang in my ears. *Seventy-two hours.* I needed more time.

The risk of becoming a vampire paled, however, at the thought of being used to open the door and allow these numbskulls to have what they so desperately desired.

Using his free hand, he gripped my hair and tugged, exposing my neck. "Open your mouth."

Fighting the lingering paralysis, I raised a trembling hand to push the container away, my attention darting to where Killion lay. I couldn't see all of him, but I saw the blood draining from his neck. Tears, hot and fierce, leaked from the corners of my eyes and trickled into my hairline. "Never."

Asteria stepped forward, grabbing my chin and forcing my mouth open. I tried to bite her, but her grip was too strong.

The still-warm liquid flowed down my throat. I gagged, unable to swallow fast enough to keep from choking. Blood splattered like a Rorschach inkblot test over Eriling's face, and he blinked, startled, then licked his lips, where a few droplets had landed.

I wanted to vomit and scream at the same time, but I could do nothing but choke.

The magic in the blood would have wiped away the last of the paralysis, but Carmilla hit me with another dose of the drug. The bliss of Killion's magic, combined with the otherworldliness of the dragon, tasted like my favorite chocolate caramel drink. It smelled of pink roses and spring rain. As I fell deeper and deeper into that bliss, my physical body succumbing to the paralytic, Eriling once more placed my hand on the stone.

Barely aware of what was going on around me, a

distant part of me screamed when the door groaned and began to slide back.

Gaining access to the crypt, Eriling dropped me on the ground, and I fell facing Killion. The blood on the floor soaked into my skin and hair. The shock of seeing him this way was exactly like Grim Zero's seeing Death lifeless. It was too much to bear.

I cried.

The others jetted into the crypt, excitement in their voices echoing off the walls. Eriling jerked the falx from its spot near the entrance before crossing the threshold.

From the corner of my eye, I watched as Thana stopped under a dragon head and yanked on it. A single bone broke off, and she giggled, holding it close to her chest. "Now, I can have everything I've ever wanted."

Ulric placed his hand on the statue, stroking the scale Andy had touched. "We can live forever."

Morag traced the original Undead's coffin, reading the inscription. "And control the future of humanity."

Over my dead body. Grim Zero gave me a punch of her energy, and I reached for Killion. Pressing my fingers against the wound on his neck was a pointless attempt to stop the bleeding, but I did it anyway.

My stomach cramped, a spasm racking my body and twisting my spine. I yelped, but the others didn't notice, so intoxicated with what they had done. I kept repeating Killion's name in my head, willing him not to die.

Eriling ran his thumb on the edge of the blade. "Only I can live forever, especially now that I have annihilated Death."

A group had gone after Death long ago, which was

why SMG had created Grim Zero—to protect him. She'd done an excellent job until someone figured out a way to trap her, remove her head, and end her existence. Eriling was a hunter, and he'd trapped the others here, not to help them achieve immortality, but to kill them.

There was nothing I could do to stop it. The blade made a hissing sound as it sliced through the air, removing Ulric's head from his neck. Blood gushed, and the separated pieces fell to the floor, his face wide-eyed with shock.

Asteria shifted into wolf form, but as she launched herself through the air to take Eriling down, he fell to a knee and sliced open her belly. She fell with a scream on top of the witch.

He made quick work of the others until Thana was the only one left, cowering under the dragon. She held out of a shaking hand, clutching the bone. "Please, I'll do whatever you—"

He plunged the end of the blood-soaked blade into her chest, stopping her words. A powerful force of magic blew out from the bone, scraping back his hair but not moving him an inch.

He turned in a circle, eyeing his work with a smile. His eyes snagged on me, watching as a wave of convulsions surged through me. My joints and limbs cracked and broke, ending up in angles they were never meant to.

He bent to run the blade through the expanding river of blood, then licked it from the metal. Kneeling beside me, he caressed my face, his own visage unnaturally beautiful and radiating with his newly enhanced power. "You and I together again, masters of life and death."

My teeth clamped down. Still, I managed to laugh. "You've screwed yourself. By killing my mate, you've sentenced me to death as well."

He stroked my bloody hair as if soothing a child. "Not true. Not for us. I possess all of this." He gestured with an open hand at the interior of the chamber. "Otherworldly magic that defies the laws of this world. I will not let you die. You will resurrect the dragons, and side by side, we will remake this realm so it serves us."

A snarl came from the shadows. A blur of black fur.

Eriling whirled at the moment the giant wolf attacked.

Killion's father was twice the size of a standard shifter and enraged as only an Undead can be. He hit Eriling with the force of the outside storm, and the two rolled into the chamber. The falx flew from his hand.

I caught the glint of an arrow as it materialized in the hunter's grip. Round two of the paralytic was beginning to wear off, and Grim Zero filled my limbs with her power. My bones and joints began to correct themselves, and I rose on hands and knees. Breathing through the agony, I lifted my hand toward the falx. It wasn't my size, but it would do.

The handle smacked into my palm, and my tattoo blazed to life. Eriling drove the arrow into the wolf's ribs, but Dragomir held on, his massive jaws clamped around the hunter's neck.

Eriling rolled and shoved the arrow deeper. Dragomir went limp. I staggered to my feet.

Was it my necromancy aiding me? Killion's blood? I

didn't know, and I didn't have time to guess. I limped into the crypt, raised the falx, and swung.

Eriling sensed what was coming right before the blade struck. He threw up an arm to block it, but it hooked into his forearm, nearly severing the limb in half. Moving at the speed of light, he ripped the arrow out of the wolf and faced me.

"Your recovery skills are unparalleled." He raised the weapon as I sunk to my knees, my legs betraying me. "Cooperate, or I will end you."

I turned up my palms in supplication. "You don't understand. I'm already dead."

He knelt, lowering the arrow. "You are the one who doesn't understand. The magical blood swirling inside you, combined with your necromancy, will keep you immortal. And once you share it with me—"

A shadow fell over us. I gasped up at the most beautiful sight I'd ever seen. Killion stood there, alive and shimmering like his dragon. He held out a hand to the falx, and as it had done for me, it soared through the air and into his palm. "You will never touch her again."

Eriling was quick, but not as quick as the dragon-fueled vampire who had taken his fill of my grim blood less than twenty-four hours before and carried the essence of the creatures who had come from another dimension. The two were a blur, but before I could suck in a breath, Eriling was sliced into three pieces and lying on the floor, eyes staring vacantly at the stalactites.

The open wound on Killion's neck had stopped bleeding, but not because he was totally drained. It was healing itself, and while his eyes were ringed with red and scales appeared and vanished over his exposed skin, I marveled at his absolute magnificence. The magical glow radiating from him ran through a spectrum of colors, his eyes locked on mine.

The light show was mesmerizing. I tried to stand and ended up on my butt. He offered a hand, and I took it, allowing him to draw me to my feet and hold me to his chest. Killion pillowed my head, and our channel opened.

Me: *I thought you were dead, for real.*

Killion: *You saved me.*

Me: *I did? How?*

Killion: *We should go upstairs. I need a drink first.*

Me: *What about this mess?*

He spoke aloud. "My father will take care of it."

I glanced at the dead wolf and saw its paws twitch. "He's not...?"

"Not yet. This wasn't how I thought it would play out, but I have to admit, his strategy worked."

Every passing minute brought me more relief. I tipped my head to look up at him and noticed the red rings were gone. "*His* strategy?"

He took my hand to lead me from the crypt, returning the weapon to its holder. "I have a lot to tell you."

TWENTY-SEVEN

Although Killion had lost all the blood, I was the one bent double from pain and debility. I only made it to the first landing before I collapsed.

He swept me up into his arms. "I'm so sorry, my love."

"I don't know what's wrong," I sputtered. "I feel like I have food poisoning."

He took the stairs two at a time, carrying me with ease. "I'm afraid it's only going to get worse."

I clung to his jacket, my nerve endings on fire. I suspected I knew the cause but hoped I was mistaken. "What's wrong with me?"

I saw the confirmation of my worst fear in his apologetic gaze. "I'll be with you through it all. This will pass, I promise."

"No, no, no." My fist beat against his chest, weak and desperate. "This can't be—"

My spine bowed with a new wave of agony.

His grip tightened, and his vampire speed kicked in as he sped up the steps.

"Stop." I breathed through the waves of pain. "Death. I have to see him. He's...dead."

Killion pivoted without argument, which surprised me, and took me to the hall. Pennyworth, Katarina, Moss, and Danesti crowded around my boss, still prone on the floor.

Katarina screwed up her nose. "What happened to you?" The question seemed directed at Killion rather than me, but when I cried out, clutching my belly, her eyes went wide. "Blood and fangs, is she...?"

His nod caused her to drop her head in what looked like submission. "I failed you both."

"We were paralyzed, thanks to Ulric," Killion said, "but as I suspected, Eriling was after the bones. He believed, rightly so, that if he possessed those, along with Chloe, he could rule over all beings. He did not succeed in his quest, even assisted by the others."

Danesti said. "Are they...?"

"Eliminated," Killion told him.

"Master," Pennyworth said, wringing his hands, "I'm afraid we don't know what to do for Death. We tried extracting the stake, but it will not come out."

"Set me down," I ordered.

He did, keeping a hand on my back to steady me.

"He can't die." I knelt next to the inert body, noting his skin was ashen, his hair white. While he didn't need to breathe, I stared at his chest, willing him to expel the gleaming stake on his own and inhale. Neither happened, and a new fear rooted itself inside me. "How is it possible that Carmilla could take him by surprise? Where was his shield? That thingy he has that protects him?"

Andy and Aurora staggered into the room, holding each other up. It was a relief to see them alive, although Aurora's skin was the same color as Death's. "Everyone was vulnerable," she said, holding her side where blood leaked through her fingers. "Because of the disintegrating spell, all magic is acting erratic and randomly backfiring."

"That's no ordinary stake," Killion added.

Danesti frowned. "Death is an actual person?"

Everybody gave him a *get with the program* look. He appeared contrite. "I overheard them discussing this overthrow, and Eriling produced the stake right before we arrived. He said it was made with a combination of good and evil. I didn't understand what he was talking about." He pointed at Death. "He said divine forces might try to intervene if he attacked you, Chloe, and this was the only weapon that could stop them."

"I thought it was dragon bone," I muttered.

Killion squatted beside me. "As close to it as you can get. That's the lead Death and I were following—the creation of that stake—but we couldn't pinpoint the origin or its maker. We assumed the animation magic was the creation of a being, not a weapon."

"There has to be something we can do." I scanned the faces around me. "We have to get that thing out of him."

Danesti leaned in for a closer look. "So he's the actual angel of death? How is it possible he can be killed?"

I glared at him. "How is it possible you're still alive after you helped Eriling?"

He blanched. "I had no choice but to play along. I warned you he was coming and that he was bringing friends."

I shot to my feet. "Warned us?" Another wave of fire ripped through my stomach. I clenched my fists. "You never said anything, you worthless coward."

Killion grabbed me. "He did warn me, Chloe. I needed to allow the group into the castle so we could overtake them when the time came. The one outlier I did not expect was Death showing up, and I certainly did not expect him to be a casualty."

"You *knew*?" It came out a screech.

"I intended to share the information and my plan with you, but they arrived sooner than anticipated. I thought they'd wait until after the storm."

"That's what they told me they would do," Danesti said. "I was as surprised as anyone when Morag showed up demanding I accompany him."

Moss shook his head. "I'm with him." He jerked his thumb at Danesti. "I don't get how Death can die."

Jerking free of Killion's hold, I dropped to my knees once more, rolling Death onto his side and tugging on the end of the stake as hard as I could. The bone buzzed with otherworldly magic, and I poured all my angst into my grip. I braced a foot against his massive back and heaved. It still didn't budge. Instead, it sent an electric shock through my arms to my chest. Every hair on my body stood on end, and I wrenched free, my heart stuttering.

Killion pulled me up. "I need to secure you in the tower. Your transformation is going to get more extreme."

"Transformation," Aurora echoed. "What are you talking about?" She scanned us, noting all the blood on our clothes and skin. A finger reached out to touch the corner of my mouth, where she wiped off a drop of it. She turned a scalding gaze on him. "You didn't! Tell me she's not beginning the change into a vampire."

"It's not his fault," I said, leaning on him. "Eriling made me drink his blood in order to access the crypt."

She put a hand to her forehead, swaying. "By the goddess, I can't believe this. What will happen to her?"

The question was directed at Killion, but I held her by the hand, trying to reassure her. "I'm going to be fine." That seemed dubious as another wave of sickness hit, and I nearly threw up on Death. I swallowed hard. If I could just stop the room spinning, I could think straight. "I need to contact SMG. They can help."

"Good idea." Killion took my elbow. "As soon as we have you restrained, I'll reach out to them." He spoke over his shoulder to Pennyworth. "We're going to need blood and lots of it."

"What about the others?" Katarina asked. She gestured between herself and Moss. "Do we need to handle clean up?"

"My father is working on it, but I'm sure he could use a hand."

Moss hung his head. "I'm sorry, Master. I should have known Thana was in on it."

None of this was his fault—or Katarina's—yet something in me wanted to lash out. "Why didn't you read her mind, Moss? Or... I don't know. Couldn't either of you sense that she was up to something?"

"Not even the guardian knew," Killion reminded me in a gentle voice. "Come. You're going to need all your strength for what comes next."

Before we took a step, Tinder appeared. A member of

Soul Management Group, he often acted as a go-between for reapers and the organization. He stared in shock at the scene, his mouth working but nothing coming out. "Bloody reaper hell," he finally murmured. His British accent was heavy. His gaze rose to mine. "So it's true, then? You failed again to protect him?"

I flinched. "I didn't know he was in danger. Grim Zero didn't warn me."

He shook his head, pushing back the sides of his tweed jacket as he placed his hands on his hips. "Mei is not going to be happy about this. I suspect you're in for a demotion, Grim 281."

Mei wasn't my biggest fan, and now, with this? I'd be lucky to survive until morning. Mostly, I felt bad about my promise to Coria.

The blizzard pelted the castle, rattling the windows so hard I thought they would break. An icy breeze swept down the stone steps and filled the hall, chilling everyone. Even Tinder glanced at the ceiling as if he could see the storm raging outside.

In the blink of an eye, the CEO herself flickered into view. She often used a form of teleportation when she didn't want to physically enter this dimension. She existed in one connected to the afterlife—a large, sprawling, endless structure filled with golden archways, marble floors, and beautiful scenery.

"I'm sorry," I said before she could speak. "I had no idea they would kill him. I didn't know what was going on."

"It's my fault," Killion told her. "I knew of the impending attack, but I kept Chloe out of the loop. It was a strategic decision, thinking I could handle it without her." I glanced at him, and he gave me a nod, encouraging me to go along with the story. "I should've known better. I wanted to keep her safe; instead, I've caused all of this."

Me: *Falling on your sword to save me from her?*

Killion: *Better me than you. All SMG can do to me is revoke my agreement with them.*

Mei barely glanced at Death, giving Killion a disapproving look. "We'll discuss that later. Death said you had something important to tell me. Something about Eriling and his mad scientist laboratory—Death's words, not mine."

I choked as the pieces fell into place. "Eriling is the one creating the soulless beings."

"Was," Killion corrected. "He'd been around long enough to figure out ways of manipulating the building blocks of life. Because of his immortality and divine origins, he decided to take all manner of creation into his own hands. Death and I discovered his ability to extract the essence of many different beings, both dead and alive, in order to make his own creatures. Diego and his sister were test subjects, but since then, Eriling had refined his magic, and we believe there are dozens of the soulless now."

A brief silence descended as we all absorbed the enormity of that. "So why did he need me?" I asked.

"Combining the bones from my ancestors and the dragons with your necromancy would make him unstoppable."

"And by eliminating Death," Mei added, "he would

truly be the most powerful being ever to exist. He could create new worlds, entirely new dimensions."

God 2.

I sagged against Killion, realizing that, even if I did become a vampire, at least we'd stopped him. "What now?" I asked Mei. "Am I on probation? Fired?"

Her always strict, solemn face was impassive. I knew I wasn't going to like what she said next, and I gripped Killion's hand where it sat on my hip. If she struck me down, he would die, too. I was preparing for the worst, even as I searched my brain for something I could offer her in exchange for his life.

Ghost bounded into the room, greeting me and Killion with her abundant energy. He lifted her from the floor and cradled her in his arm, his protective magic wrapping around us. He knew what I was thinking and what the consequences would be if Mei decided I was responsible for my boss' demise.

Her image flickered again, and I wondered if the storm had anything to do with it or if she was as eager to get out of the situation as I was. "Until the board of directors can meet and decide on a way forward, you will take his place."

The silence this time was much, much longer. All eyes landed on me.

Tinder chuckled. "You're kidding, eh, boss?"

"I'm sorry." I shook my head to try and clear the buzzing in my ears. "It sounded like you're saying I'm now...Death."

"This is a unique situation, but the rules for reapers are clear." She sighed, disgusted. "Just like when you terminated Gustafson, you're obligated to take Death's place for a term of three hundred and sixty-five days." She cast a somewhat defeated glance at my boss. My *former* boss. "Tinder will provide you with the paperwork, and I'll be in contact with your orders within the next forty-eight hours. See if you can stay out of trouble for that long."

She vanished, and Tinder opened his hand. The logbook listing grim reapers appeared in it. "Congratulations, Grim 281," he said. "You've been promoted to Death 2."

TWENTY-EIGHT

Three days. That was the amount of time lost to me during the transition.

Agony was my constant companion, a monster who held me between rows of jagged teeth. My mind disassociated from my body at times, and I experienced strange hallucinations and horror-filled nightmares.

What's new?

I dreamed of Death cracking open his chest to show me the heart inside with a gaping hole in it. Next to it was the place where his soul should reside, which was now empty.

He was furious with me for failing him and demanded I make his heart beat again. He ordered me to return his soul and raise him from the dead whom he ruled over.

Another nightmare took me to the beginning of time, where I saw through the eyes of what I could only guess was Xychel, one of the first Undead to enter this dimension. Death stood before a swirling portal of energy, causing it to close. "You're unnatural. You do not belong here," he told Killion's forebearer, "and I will not allow any more of your kind into this dimension."

When Death moved across the landscape, everything withered and died, but a female with him—Grim Zero—trailed in his wake, bringing life back to all the plants, trees, and animals.

He touched Xychel, trying to kill him, but it didn't work. Xychel sneered in his face.

Never had anything surprised Death. Never had anyone defied him. He labeled them the Undead and vowed to wipe them out, no matter what it took or how long.

Killion held me through all of it, using his magic to attempt to soothe and console me. It didn't work, although I tried to hold in the worst of it. I knew he suffered with me, only he had learned long ago how to handle pain.

The blood he'd ordered was not for me but for him. He expected I would feed off of him as all new vampires are ravenous and must feed from their sire, but I had no stomach for it. I wasn't normal, and my transition did not cause bloodlust—just the opposite. The one time I succumbed to accepting nourishment, I ended up vomiting it back up.

We discussed his parentage and the revelations about his mother. At some point, Dragomir visited, and Killion went to the outer chamber to talk to him. He confirmed Coria was attached to the atrium, and he to her. I didn't mention my promise to her, but I couldn't block Killion from reading my thoughts.

I ran hot and cold, vacillating between the sensation of my blood boiling in my veins and then freezing. When I was burning up, he carried me out into the snow, where I melted it, clearing three-foot-deep piles down to the bare ground. When my blood switched to ice, he bundled us in blankets in front of a roaring fire.

During a lucid moment, I remember snuggling against his chest as we lay in bed. "What do you want?" he asked. "Tell me what will bring you relief, no matter what it is, and I will get it for you."

Delirious and feeling as though I had lost some part of me, I said the first thing that popped into my head. "I want a unicorn."

"What?"

"You heard me. They say the horn is magical; if you rub it, the unicorn will grant you a wish. Outside of that, I don't know anything that can help me feel like myself again."

I sensed his desperation and disappointment. "If possible, I would turn into one myself for you."

"Would I have to stroke your horn in order to get you to grant my wish?"

He chuckled at the innuendo. "Most certainly."

When it was over, I woke to find myself five pounds lighter, my hair thicker, and my eyesight sharper. A part of me had died and been reborn, and there was something I had to do.

His violet eyes watched as I scrubbed myself clean in the enormous tub. Once finished, I accepted the towel he handed me. He said little as I dressed in some of Katarina's goth clothes, the channel between us now an ocean. I didn't need to read his mind to know his thoughts—he was unsure what I was and could do.

A tribrid: part grim, part Undead, and part Fae.

He'd accepted the fact that he was not part-human as he'd been led to believe, and yet, he struggled to wrap his mind around it. The issue surrounding whether he had a soul or not remained.

The storm dissipated; Aurora created a new pact between the witch coven, shifter clans, and vampires to keep peace in the territory. Killion made her and Andy his liaisons, granting them the power of his station to pick who would enforce it before he sealed it with his blood.

After an enormous breakfast in the atrium, I marched to the cold storage room where the others had placed Death's body. Killion followed. No one understood why SMG hadn't taken Death, but even without the cool temperature of the room, I imagined he would stay in stasis forever. He deserved a proper burial, but I had no clue where he might want to be laid to rest, and I had an entirely different idea.

Katarina hovered at the door, awaiting instructions from Killion. He eyed me with curious speculation. I shooed her away. "Leave."

As expected, she bristled. "You've become insufferable, you know that?"

I met her angry stare. "You're the enforcer for the most powerful Undead master ever to walk this earth. Stop being petty and start acting like it."

Her eyes grew wide, and I thought she might attack

me. Instead, she grinned. "Are you sure you're not a vampire?"

No one could believe that I didn't crave blood. "I can tell you don't have a heartbeat, and I bet I can beat you in hand-to-hand combat now. As soon as I take care of this, in fact, I'm game to try. If you think you're up for it," I added.

She flashed her fangs. "Good to have you back, Grave Girl."

I returned the smile, making sure she saw that I did not have elongated incisors. That wouldn't stop me from kicking her Undead butt.

After she disappeared, Killion drew me away from the body. "Please tell me you're not about to do what I think you're going to."

"Do you really want me to take his place?"

Of course he didn't. Yet, he was concerned about what might happen if I did. Once I committed, there was no reneging. "This has never been done. What if it backfires?"

I squeezed his hand. "I'll handle it."

He sighed, a reluctant sound that shimmered between us. His energy seemed to be normal, but I felt a weirdness in his mind. It had been a memorable few days, and the revelations about his mother and father, as well as the events leading to my transition, had worn him down. "I have no doubt of that, but will it bring you peace?" he asked. "If not, are you sure it will be worth it?"

From what I had discovered, there was no true peace in this world. Only the shift into the afterlife could bring that. "There is more to Grim Zero than what any of us have been told. I understand that now, and I know what her true role was designed to be."

I saw the instant he grasped my meaning. "She wasn't his protector."

I shook my head and refocused on Death. "In the event of a catastrophe such as this, she was created to bring him back. That's why her necromancy is so strong." I allowed the memory of what I'd seen at the beginning of time to unfurl for him.

His shoulders sagged under the weight of this latest revelation. "Chloe, can you do it?"

I gave him a saucy smile, a part of the old me surfacing. "Can you imagine Death's face when he wakes up and sees me? When he realizes what happened and that he'll be indebted to me forever for resurrecting him?"

Killion chuckled. "A silver lining? The glass half full?"

More than that, it was going to give me a new level of power with SMG that could change everything for us. This kind of power was heady, and I knew they needed to keep checks and balances on me, but in the days to come, we'd figure it out. "I need to know that you're okay with this. We're partners, and you're better at strategy than I am. I know there will be consequences, and while Death isn't perfect, he's an expert at his job. I don't want this promotion, and we all know I'm not the person for it."

He went quiet, and I had a front-row seat as his brilliant mind analyzed all the possible outcomes along with the fallout from each. Eventually, he braced his hands on the table, where Death lay, a muscle in his jaw feathering before he said, "There is no 'best option' under the circumstances. Whatever comes, comes."

I crooked a brow. "We'll handle it?"

"While our bond was unbreakable before, it is now something that even I cannot fully comprehend." He came around the table and embraced me." You have become something that is too much for this world. I don't know what the future holds for you, for us, but I will be there by your side every step of the way."

I touched his cheek and felt an enormous chasm of the unknown open underneath our feet. A part of me longed to return to being Chloe Frost. I wanted to marry him and live in Danté's Grove. Run my clinic, hang out with my friends. Have a family. I wanted to forget about the supernatural world and all the things that happened to me since I had taken up the reaper's robes.

That was one path that would never be available to me again. I had become a monster in this world, and there was no going back. There was no normal for me anymore. All the things that had been important to me had become background noise to what lay before me. "We have Eriling's creations to hunt down and others to protect. You have an empire to run, and I have other options to explore."

He misunderstood. "Leaving me, are you?"

"Ha. Yeah, no. I meant that, together, we have wrongs to right, mysteries to dig into, and SMG is several millennia overdue for restructuring. Think you're up for it, fang boy?"

The teasing nickname made his shoulders relax, but I saw a weariness in his eyes. "Restructuring?"

I kissed him and withdrew from his hold. "We can talk about it after we discuss that unicorn you're going to turn into. You did promise, right?"

He offered a cheeky smile. "You only wish to stroke my horn."

An instant flash of lust rippled through me and I licked my lips. His eyes were drawn to them, and he pushed an image into my mind of the two of us enjoying our honeymoon.

The wedding, right. With everything going on, I'd completely forgotten about it.

While the storm here had cleared, the North American East Coast was struggling through a horrendous blizzard. There was still no way for them to arrive in time nor for the seamstress to bring me a new gown. I'd have to think about that later as well.

I pushed a few of my own visuals at him, the spot between my legs tingling. I touched his mother's ring, remembering her request. "How many days until Christmas?"

"We can hold a ceremony whenever you want. Nothing says we have to stick to that day after everything you've been through."

I turned that over in my head, considering where else might be a better venue, but I knew this was the right one. "I want a midnight ceremony on Christmas Eve. At the stroke of midnight, on Christmas Day, I want to be Mrs. Killion Reveux. Okay?"

His smile turned satisfied. "I can think of no better present."

Neither could I. We stood across the table from each

other, and I reached for his hand. He took it, and then we each touched Death.

As a rookie reaper, my necromancy had felt like a separate limb, awkward and repulsive, even after I became friendly with Grim Zero. During the transition of becoming Undead, she'd disappeared. At first, I thought it was because Death had perished, and they were bound like Killion and I. If one died, so did the other.

But as I tapped into my life-giving magic, I felt her brush against my heart. Opening up to her power was as easy as running my fingers under a water faucet, feeling her energy flow over me and out to him. She was a new plant bursting through the soil and reaching for him, her sun.

Killion felt it, too, his hand tightening on mine. I closed my eyes and sent tendrils searching for whatever soul Death had been embodied with. It seemed to be all around me, under me, above me, his divine power in everything that existed. I sensed it even in this castle, in the stones, in the wood, and the bones below us.

It seemed that despite the fact the original Undead had come from a dimension where he had no dominion, they had still eventually succumbed to this one where he did. There truly was no escaping him.

Ghost bounded into the room, barking and shifting into her psychopomp form. The floorboards shook, the walls trembled, and my hair stood on end.

I didn't stop, didn't retreat. I drew it toward me, relishing it as the ultimate power raced through my system.

My head snapped back, my body arching from the intensity of it. Together, we channeled the power into the lifeless form we gripped, and the room around us exploded in light and magic.

In the aftermath, when I could open my eyes and take in what had happened, I found that the furniture, pictures, and other assorted items had been reduced to dust at our feet. There was no longer a corpse on the table, but I heard Death's voice.

"For reaper's sake," he grumbled, his spectral body floating a few feet away as he looked down at himself and then at me.

"Hey, boss." I bit my bottom lip, watching his ethereal form. This wasn't good. "Welcome back."

"What have you done?" he growled.

"No big deal." He was going to kill me, no doubt about it. "I think I just turned you into a ghost."

TWENTY-NINE

The castle came alive in a new way during the following days in anticipation of the wedding. An assortment of beautiful decorations appeared in amethyst and magenta in place of the traditional Christmas colors.

Fresh pine boughs, pinecones, and cranberries were wound into long garlands that covered every surface. The largest wreath I'd ever seen appeared in the Great Hall over the fireplace. Scented candles burned day and night, filling the musty air with a refreshing combination of cedar, spruce, and cinnamon.

Harmony appeared one morning while I luxuriated in the bath. As the Fae could do from her dimension, she simply opened a portal between the worlds and stepped through, planking on the edge of the large tub. Her long blond hair hung in two braids, and she wore a large magnolia leaf as a skirt and flower petals over her nipples. "You turned my boyfriend into a ghost."

She had a huge crush on Death. Shocked, I sat up quickly, pulling bubbles toward me for cover. "We're working on it. He'll be back to normal soon." At least, he might be. As far as we knew, SMG had not determined how to create a new body for him since he was not and never had been exactly human. "What are you doing here?"

She glanced at the portal. "I brought your dress."

Estrid, Killion's beloved seamstress, entered, eyeballing the door and the two of us. She was a short vampire with a no-nonsense attitude.

She glared down her nose at me before snapping her fingers at her lurking assistant, who was twice her size and carrying a trunk. "You are ready?" she asked me.

Sinking deeper into the water, I pointed at the bedroom and castle beyond. "Pennyworth is around. He'll show you where to go."

The two of them left, and I stared at Harmony, waiting for her to go as well. She didn't. Instead, she peered into the bathwater. "Got room for me?"

The Fae were comfortable with their bodies, and they had no qualms about sexuality or relationships. I shook my head. "I was just finishing. There are plenty of other tubs in the castle, and I'm happy to have someone draw you a bath if you want."

She sighed dramatically. "It's really no fun unless you have a partner to play with." She eyed me expectantly. "You *will* fix him, right? I mean, you're some freaky supernatural now."

Word gets around quickly in the supernatural

community, just like the human one. *Freaky supernatural. That's me.* "Of course," I lied. In my opinion, there was no fixing Death, even if we restored him to a physical body. "Say, do you know anything about the Forest Fae?"

She screwed up her nose. "Not my crowd."

Killion and I had had more discussions about his heritage, what to do with his mother and father, and how we could convince SMG to view their soulmate bond as restoring universal balance. I'd put in the request for Coria to be reincarnated and returned to Dragomir, but so far, Mei had been mute about it. I'd reminded her that Dragomir had taken on Eriling and helped stop him. That alone should give him bonus points in the 'universal balance' column. "If I restore Death to the way he was, I might need to call in a favor."

This piqued her curiosity. "Are you talking about a fairy bargain?"

Maybe. I might need a sanctuary for Killion's parents, and while she and her father would be opposed to providing it, I'd pulled off more complicated tasks. "How badly do you want a date with Death?"

Her laughter sounded like delicate windchimes with the underlying purr of a lion. She flicked water at me. "Throw in a bubble bath and I'd do just about anything for you."

I held out a wet hand. "Done."

We shook, and I motioned toward the portal she'd created. "I'll let you know as soon as he's back. See you later."

She stretched lazily, the portal closing. "Oh, I'm not going anywhere. I'm here for the ceremony." She paused at the bathroom door, and I swear I saw butterflies flittering around her fingers as she ran a hand over the solid wood. Glancing back, she grinned at me. "I just love a good wedding."

While my family and friends couldn't make it, Katarina had rigged a live feed so they could watch from the comfort of their homes in Danté's Grove. I was relieved about that, even though Uncle Morty wouldn't be able to walk me down the aisle and give me away. I'd considered asking Pennyworth, and I knew he'd be thrilled, but something didn't feel right about it.

I wandered the castle, feeling more like myself, and peeked in a few times to the Hall to marvel at the transformation. He'd turned it from a stark, depressing room into a festive and happy place.

Killion had been in meetings with the local heads of supernatural communities for the past two days while I worked on getting my bearings with my enhanced abilities. None of us had any idea how powerful I was now, and while I had managed to knock Katarina flat during our last training session, in truth, I'd been holding back.

Grim Zero's power had always felt like a bottomless pit. Although I had no desire to drink blood, and I wasn't showing signs of having fangs, the mix of magics felt alien. Like Death, Grim Zero had been created from the cosmos with stardust and other elements I couldn't name. The otherworldly magic of Killion's line gnawed at that cosmic magic as though it wanted to consume it.

I'd never questioned him about how many vampires he'd sired. After my transformation, I'd finally gathered the courage to, hoping that one of them might still be around. I wanted to know what they'd experienced and if what I felt was normal.

"The originals and their progeny created many Undead," he'd explained, "and as I explained, those Undead created the line of vampires who walk the earth today. But none of them have been sired by me. You are the only one I have ever turned."

That fact struck me hard. "But the power your family amassed was partly due to how many followers they had."

He nodded. "Every vampire who exists could potentially claim the originals as a sire. It's the same for humans tracing their ancestry to the first mortal man and woman. The amount of magic they possess is such a small fraction of what I do, it's insignificant."

"Why didn't you turn anybody?"

We'd been looking out over the courtyard from the balcony. He'd pulled me close, and I'd laid my head on his shoulder. "There are far too many vampires in the world. They need guidance, not more competition. Many rogues kill humans unchecked, and due to their inability to control themselves, they could potentially wipe out the human population. What good would that do us?"

"And your father?"

"He killed plenty of humans and supernaturals, but to the best of my knowledge, his army followed him because he protected them and wanted to eradicate the vampire gangs who sought to destroy this world. The only entity he wanted to turn was my mother, and she would not allow it."

"Would it have even been possible? Because of her heritage?"

"I guess we'll never know."

"You nearly drained me to the brink of death that night, and although there's no transformation to become a grim like there is a vampire, do you feel any different? You're as much a tribrid as I am, right?"

"I don't believe it works that way. I am Undead and Forest Fae—a rare combination. A unicorn, you might say." When I pulled back to grin up at him, he winked. "And while our bond allows me to touch your magic and benefit from it, the essence of Grim Zero is not carried in your blood. It's here." He tapped my heart. "She's absorbed the Undead magic in your veins, and it's likely that the enhanced powers you've displayed since aren't because I turned you."

"Then what?"

"The transformation allowed you to access her power more fully."

I braced my hands on the railing, letting that sink in. "So I'm not a tribrid?"

"You are." He stood next to me, staring at the landscape. "But I suspect you'll only acquire the skills you desire—that's your true power."

No fangs. No blood lust. But plenty of strength, speed, and enhanced senses. I could live with that. The one chink in that theory seemed to be with the otherworldly magic that Killion had transferred to me. A fiery burn in my veins never seemed to go out. As if I now had the dragon's essence inside me. If I overexerted myself while upset or angry, like in my training sessions with Katarina, it exploded out of me with a vengeance.

Our sessions had always been antagonistic at best. I

could never quite determine if we were friends or not, and she was the most competitive being I'd ever encountered. She sought to win at all costs, and with my new cocktail of magics, she had gone all out to test my abilities. I had this unnerving feeling that I could literally spit fire if I wanted to. When Killion and I took his mother's remains into the woods, I was going to experiment with turning the fire loose. He could ensure no animals or occupants were around, and I could relax about hurting anybody.

I hadn't told him that yet and hoped he would understand. I'd tried using our connection to see if he sensed the dragon fire in his own veins, but I assumed it didn't feel odd to him after living with it his whole life. I had been reluctant to allow any thoughts about it into my mind in case he was listening, but I had to know. I couldn't risk going home and accidentally harming a friend or family member. Or burning down the entire town.

I stopped inside the atrium, seeking Coria. Ghost came running down the path, greeting me, and as I lifted her, I sensed Killion's father drawing near. Even with a cosmic well of power inside me, I had to fight my instinct not to step back when he appeared, scowling as usual.

"She's as bullheaded in death as she was in life." He turned to look at the tree, crossing his arms over his chest. "She wants you to return her to the forest."

"I know. She never loved anyone but you, though, and the bond you shared will never break, even in the afterlife."

He grunted. "There is no afterlife for me. It's just... oblivion."

"Maybe not. Will you stay here in the castle or abandon it for the woods once she's returned to her family?"

He turned slowly, appraising me. "You're giving me a choice?"

"I happen to be a valuable employee of Soul Management Group. Until my boss is officially reinstated, I hold discretion over life and death in this dimension. I'm not sure you deserve compassion or grace, but I'm offering you an opportunity to prove that you're worthy of it going forward."

His return stare was calculating but curious. "I'm listening."

"SMG moves slowly, and the head of the organization is not my fan. She's proven to be fair, but only when it comes to following the laws of universal balance. It seems to me that many things in this universe are not balanced, and this is one of them. Like the vampires who've roamed the Earth unchecked and out of control, wishing to bring down the originals and create chaos. I fear the soulless beings Eriling created, who are now leaderless, will choose a similar path. I'm looking for hunters to bring them in."

"No," he said without hesitation. "You're not offering me freedom, only a new set of chains."

Who was bullheaded now? "There are approximately a dozen of them, and I will take steps to ensure that no other beings like them are ever created. Once we terminate them, you'll have your freedom."

"And my son?"

"What about him?"

"He's agreeable to this offer?"

"I haven't spoken to him about it." But the channel between us was open and he was listening. I waited for any objection he might send. None came. "I believe he will be agreeable, but we can speak to him now if you want."

"You're smart. Cunning."

"Will you do it?"

"I'll think about it." He scratched behind Ghost's ear. "When you die, will you be buried with him?"

The dog wriggled in my arms, straining to lick his hand. "Here, you mean? With your ancestors? That's not allowed."

He lifted Ghost from me and cuddled her. An unnerving sight. "Thought you wanted to change the rules."

So Killion had told him that.

The fan girl my dog turned into around Killion extended to his father. The fact she was a good judge of character made me less antagonistic toward him. "Are you okay with that?"

"He's stated to me that he doesn't wish to be entombed with the rest of us, but because of his heritage, you understand why it's critical he not be buried elsewhere."

"Yes, I know." I tipped my head to the looming forest. I had no desire to be buried here either, yet he was right—Killion's bones were pure magic, Undead and Fae. I thought of his heartbeat, the reassuring sound that lulled me to sleep every night, and the idea of it no longer beating. My chest tightened. I had planned to be laid to rest next to my parents in Danté's Grove, but now... "He and I will determine the best course of action for each of us."

"Shaking up those rules again?"

I shrugged. "What's life without a little excitement?"

"You're one of us now," he stroked the dog's fur absentmindedly. "If you so choose to be buried with him, I won't keep you out of our sacred crypt."

Shock made my mouth fall open. I snapped it shut. "Come on," I teased, "you like me, and you know it."

He placed Ghost on the floor, and she raced around our feet, barking to incite a game. He lunged at her, and I sucked in a breath, but she loved it, racing down the path before turning to rush back and growl at him. He chuckled. "You're growing on me."

It wasn't exactly a "welcome to the family," but it felt like progress.

"Whose bones are in your crypt?" I'd meant to ask Killion. "The ones that are supposedly yours."

He hesitated, then shrugged. "There was a child before Constantine. Coria miscarried early in the pregnancy. She begged me to bury our daughter in the woods, and I did. Once I came back, however, I couldn't bear the thought of her out there, all alone. There is a grotto, a natural cave. I placed a memorial there to honor her Fae heritage and secured her bones in my tomb."

I sensed Killion's shock. Sadness wormed its way into my heart. "What was her name?"

"Everbe." He cleared his throat.

"Ever Be? That poem..." At his nod, I smiled. Killion

had read it to me, along with so many others Dragomir had written to Coria. I'd assumed that one had also been for his soulmate—now I understood it was an ode to their child. "'*No matter the days I have yet to see, you will ever be with me,*'" I quoted.

A muscle in his jaw feathered with restrained emotion. "I spend time every day down there. Every full moon, I read it to her."

"It's beautiful. I can't imagine how awful it is to lose a child." He simply nodded, his throat working with emotion. We were quiet for a long moment, but Ghost snapped us out of our melancholy. She danced at our feet, turning circles and sitting on her hind legs. "One more thing," I said to him, watching her. "I need a favor."

He lunged at her, sending her jetting off again into the depths of plants, barking happily. "What is it?"

I caught the briefest glance of Coria eavesdropping on us behind the tree and smiling as she watched the dog's antics. "My father passed several years ago, and my uncle can't be here for the ceremony. I need someone to walk me down the aisle tonight."

His shock was extraordinary, and it made me laugh. "You don't seem the type to need anyone for such a traditional, matriarchal ritual," he grumbled.

"It would mean a lot to me, and I believe, to your son. This is your home, and it would be one small way for you to atone for all the crap you did to him when he was growing up."

Again, his shock was apparent. "You don't even like me."

"My dog does, and right now, that's good enough.

Stay in my good graces, okay? That's all I'm asking. Your son is incredible, and you're lucky to get a second chance with him. I'd give anything to have my parents back, so don't waste this."

I whistled for Ghost, and she bounded out of a group of philodendrons. I scooped her up and marched out, leaving him speechless.

THIRTY

To Pennyworth's dismay, I decided to move the ceremony into the atrium. It was warm and full of life and felt like the perfect place for new beginnings.

Being the competent vampire he was, he swiftly shifted the candles and garland there while Katarina cursed me out for having to set up the live feed all over again in a place with limited room for the cameras and audio equipment.

Estrid designated the library as the dressing room, and once I was in the new gown, I chased her and Aurora out so I could have a moment alone. In front of the free-standing cheval mirror, I ran a hand over the rich purple fabric that clung to my curves. She'd done a magical job remaking my dream dress in such a short time. I sashayed around, enjoying how the inserts flared as I strutted.

A tear escaped my eye, thinking about what it would've been like if my mother had been present to fuss over me and offer advice before I said my vows. It wasn't the wedding I'd long fantasized about, but it was still the happiest day of my life in so many ways.

"You look stunning." I whirled to find Death sitting in a chair in the corner. He appeared to be his usual self.

"You're back! Like, all of you."

"Don't ask me how. One minute I was a ghost, and the next..." He held up his hands. "Here I am."

"What a relief. I was afraid Mei would hold me to becoming Death 2."

He stood, his gaze skimming over my dress. "You're not off the hook yet. Things are...in turmoil up there." He pointed toward the heavens. "They don't know what to do with you. I suggest you keep your head down and do what they say."

"What are they going to do to me if I don't?"

He shrugged, not meeting my eyes. "Best not to antagonize them until things cool down."

"I could never take your place, you know. I don't want to."

"Doubt that." His grin was weak. "You've surpassed all my expectations—and theirs, too." He pointed up again. "We both know the truth now about Grim Zero and her purpose."

We did, indeed. "How could SMG not realize it?"

"There are plenty of mysteries in the universe." He smoothed back his hair, still a shocking white. "But let's get something straight—no more dying for either of us, got it? I'm sick of death."

The irony wasn't lost on me. "I'm afraid it's part of our job."

"I hope you're happy," he said. "With him." He

strolled toward the door, and it wasn't until that moment I realized he was wearing a suit.

"Are you staying for the ceremony?"

He paused with his hand on the knob. "Not sure yet." He glanced back. "It's not easy for me to watch you marry him, you know."

My heart gave a tug. Grim Zero reached for him. "It would make me happy if you stayed."

The sadness lifted a bit. "Yeah?"

I smiled. "If you're up for it, I have a job for you. Walk me down the aisle?"

The corners of his eyes narrowed, wary. "You can't be serious."

I sidled up to him and linked my arm through his. "Serious as Death."

He cringed.

"Too early?" I asked.

"You think?"

"If you don't want to participate, you can sit with Harmony. She'll be delighted."

His face turned all shades of red. "Harmony? Gods, tell me she's not here."

I chuckled. "Oh, she's here and looking for a bubble bath partner. Don't make me sic her on you."

His broad shoulders sagged. "I'll do whatever you want, just keep her away from me."

ALTHOUGH NEITHER MY dad nor Uncle Morty walked me down the aisle, I had two powerful supernatural males to take their place—Dragomir on one side and Death on the other.

The path to the atrium had a violet runner that matched Killion's eyes and was strewn with rose petals. Everyone stood when Pennyworth and Omwee pushed open the glass doors to allow us entry. Katarina shifted the camera to make sure we were in the shot as we moved in step with the music.

Ghost greeted us, and I took a moment to pat her head. Killion, dressed in a tux shipped in from a Swedish designer weeks ago, stood waiting under the tree. My breath lodged in my chest at the sight of him, and his cool, calm demeanor zeroed in on me, causing the blood inside me to rise with a fiery intensity. He barely glanced at Death or acknowledged he was no longer a ghost.

I stumbled and came to a halt, my escorts nearly tripping.

Killion: *Breathe, my love. You're doing great. Come to me, now.*

Me: *I can't believe this is happening.*

Killion: *Cold feet?*

Me: *Never.*

With renewed determination, I moved with grace toward him, my escorts barely able to stay even with me. The path was too narrow for their equally massive bodies, but we managed. When we reached the tree, each kissed my cheek before fading into the small crowd.

Aurora, acting as our officiant, smiled. Andy was off to Killion's side, acting as his sole groomsman. Floating across from the two males, barely visible, was Coria. Her gaze flicked to me, and she nodded, pleased to be included as my matron of honor.

"I am speechless," Killion said, taking my hands in his.

"I hope not." Aurora removed the sash and began binding our hands together. "It's time to say your vows."

A few people chuckled. She cleared her throat. "We gather here tonight, under the full moon of Yuletide, to unite these two souls in physical matrimony. They are already bound throughout time and space, but they wish to make a formal declaration to each other, with us as witnesses." She rested her hands on our wrists. "Killion, your vows?"

He squeezed my fingers, that faint smile I loved crossing his lips. "In the moon's embrace, under the veil of night, I pledge to you eternity. With immortal devotion, I bind my soul to yours in darkness and light. From this moment forth, we reign as one, eternally entwined. With blood and passion, I vow to love you, Chloe Frost, as my eternal bride."

There was a collective sigh inside my head and in the room. Now, who was speechless?

"Chloe," Aurora said, "your reply?"

I hadn't written up anything formal. Even if I had, it wouldn't have held a candle to his.

I glanced at those gathered. Harmony had scooted her chair beside Death's and wound her arm through his. Moss stood to the side and gave me a solemn nod. Omwee had an arm around a crying Pennyworth, and Katarina gave me a thumbs-up from behind the camera.

Dragomir sat at the back, and I thought there was a hint of pride on his face as he looked at his son.

"Most of you know I'm not good with words, but there's nowhere I'd rather be at this moment and no one I'd rather be with." I cleared my throat, emotions choking it. "When I was eighteen, my parents died," I said, "and I wanted to die, too." Technically, I had, but I had resurrected myself without realizing who and what I was. "As fate would have it, I lived, and now I know why." I faced Killion. "Because I needed to find my soulmate."

He squeezed my fingers again.

I battled back tears. "Killion, to you, I pledge my life and my heart, and even when Death's embrace comes, my soul will be yours, always and forever."

"In this life and the next," he murmured so softly only I heard it.

It had always been our pledge to each other. I nodded. "In this life and the next."

Aurora rearranged the sash to bind his right hand with my left and gently turned us to face the camera and onlookers. "I now declare Killion Reveux and Chloe Frost bound in marriage." She leaned in and lowered her voice. "You may kiss your betrothed."

It was a kiss for the ages. For the storybooks.

A bond of universal forces that would transcend this life and everything that came afterward.

EPILOGUE

*D*anté's Grove
Forty-eight hours later

KILLION ASSISTED me from the limo. I was so happy to return to home that I wanted to kiss the ground.

I nearly threw my arms around the valet, who stepped forward to help us with our luggage at the hotel. Moss waved him off and did the job. Once we were inside, he bid us goodnight; it felt like we'd been gone for months rather than a few weeks.

Ghost was happy to be home, too, racing from room to room and inventorying her beds, toys, and bowls. I found myself humming as I unpacked my dress and hung it up. It wasn't exactly something I would wear many places, but Nita insisted we hold a reception in town for the friends and family who hadn't made it to the ceremony. I would wear it to that.

On the way home, I had fielded dozens of calls from her, my aunt and uncle, my former landlady, Vera, and others. The live stream had been a hit, and they all wanted copies. Most wanted to know where we were going on our honeymoon and seemed disappointed when I explained we were coming home. They brightened when I mentioned the reception.

For me, there was no better way to start my married life than alone time with Killion. We'd discussed taking a whirlwind tour of Europe's most significant cities or possibly a cruise. After what we'd been through, we both were ready for peace and quiet.

I was due to take my veterinary board certification in mid-January, and I would put in the necessary hours of study after the first of the year. In some ways, it seemed inconsequential, but I wanted to fill my parents' shoes. I was undoubtedly keeping my clinic.

Until then, I had other things to sort out regarding my reaper duties and capturing Eriling's creatures—The Twelve, as I had dubbed them. Dragomir and Death were already on the hunt, and I anticipated that Killion and I would be flying here and there when necessary to make sure we caught every one of them before they unleashed serious damage to humans.

Our trip to the woods before we left had been a solemn one. We'd found a clearing on a hill surrounded by cedar trees to leave his mother's remains, including the stolen bone. His father had gathered Killion's sister's as well and gone with us to say a few words in an ancient language that spoke of his love for both of them. I'd dashed tears away and watched Coria's spirit dance into the trees with a tiny one held in her arms.

I'd confessed to Killion about the fiery magic I felt in my veins. He'd told Dragomir. The elder male had insisted it was a gift, but I wasn't so sure. While I followed them to a cave in the mountainside and tried to access it, all I managed to do was cause a mild avalanche that nearly trapped us inside. Grim Zero had cracked her knuckles and grinned, and I swear I heard Killion's inner dragon snort. The experience unnerved me enough that I decided to leave it alone for the time being. Killion assured me he'd train me to handle the power with confidence in the coming months.

Ensconced once more at the penthouse, I wasn't surprised when Pennyworth knocked at the door and offered to make us a meal. Killion gave him the night off, and we ordered room service instead. Once dinner was delivered, we escaped into the bedroom to feed each other—in more ways than one.

That night, in bed, I lay my head on my mate's chest to listen to his heartbeat. A sense of peace crept through my body. "I love you," I said.

He shifted to pull me under him and stared into my eyes. "What you have done for me and my family, I can never repay."

I slid my fingers into his hair and tugged his mouth to mine. "I won't complain if you try. Let's see...I can think of several ways to start paying off your debt right now."

He tickled my side, and I laughed. His lips trailed down my collarbone and went lower. "I'll do my best."

His best was pretty darn good. I sucked in my breath

when he found the sweet spot between my legs. "Good thing you have an eternity to work on it."

"Good thing," he said, and then he made me lose all rational thought.

Except for the one he sent down our channel...

In this life and the next.

THANK you for reading Grim Vows, The Accidental Reaper Series, Book 6. This story took me on a wonderful ride full of adventure, and I hope it did the same for you!

Don't miss *Undead Ever After*, the next Chloe and Killion story, coming in 2025.

***

AS A GIFT for reading this story, I'm offering a huge discount on **The Accidental Reaper Paranormal Urban Fantasy Series Special Collection: Books 1 & 2 With Bonus Story**. You can read Reaper's Keepers PLUS a bonus story not available at retailers!

IF YOU CAN'T GET ENOUGH **of Chloe, Killion, Death, and Ghost, join my VIP subscription community!** My paid VIPs get episodes in the Grim-

Verse that you can't read anywhere else. It's only $5 a month. Give it a try!

I'm in! Give me more stories!

Start Grim & Bare It in Killion's POV right now!

Episode 1 – Killion sees Chloe for the first time

THE STREETS GLISTENED LIKE ONYX, slick with rain. The cloying odor of dank alleys and wet leaves clouded the air. Humans were few and far between on this street, the drizzly night dampening the turnout for the parade a few blocks over. Only brave—or drunk— souls wandered about, unaware of those like me who hunted them. The rest listened to their survival instincts and stayed inside.

With an unusual exception.

A hundred yards away, a young woman flicked the beam of her flashlight under bushes and up into skeletal tree branches, searching for something. A lost cat, if my mind-reading skills were accurate. They were, but her thoughts were chaotic and disorderly, a deluge of random facts, conversations, and ideas: The cat's name, the bath she'd abandoned to come search for it, annoyance with her landlady, her work schedule...it went on and on.

One of the things I found fascinating about

mundanes—humans without magic—was their penchant to survive against all odds. Examples like this woman proved my point—they were rarely able to hold a single thought for more than seventeen seconds. After three hundred years as a half-vampire, half-human hybrid, I'd tracked this and other minutiae about them.

In my youth, I had been fixated on what made humans *human*. I'd wished to fit in somewhere, being neither fully like them, nor like my Undead father, descended from a long line of elite vampires. Yet, I'd found no tell-tale secrets or hidden keys to unlock the mystery. Humans were the most imperfect species I'd ever met.

This female in particular was...interesting.

"The perfect night for a murder," she murmured, peering down into a ditch.

Indeed it was.

My heightened senses zeroed in on her from my seat at the table outside Boozy's Bar, her low, smoky voice sending a sense of recognition through me. Yet, I was sure we'd never met. My nostrils flared, inhaling her scent. Under her shampoo and the lingering bath salts, I smelled...coffee grounds?

Perhaps that's why she triggered the idea I knew her. While being half-vampire required me to drink blood, I also enjoyed mundane food, such as coffee. I took in her wet hair, jacket slick with rain, and her pale face. Nothing about her features registered with me. Was she someone from my past? Had she changed her appearance? I breathed deeper.

She called the cat's name, offering a treat. Her intoxicating scent, combined with that sexy voice, made me reel. The essence of it danced at the edges of my awareness, teasing, taunting. I couldn't name it, yet it tugged at something deep and ancient inside me. She wasn't mundane, though her appearance and scattered mental energy suggested differently.

I had instinctively cataloged every supernatural I'd ever met, and now my mind raced through them, attempting to pinpoint classification, breed, and genus.

I came up blank.

She was more than interesting. She was...

Nothing I'd ever encountered before.

In three hundred years of experiences from all around the world, that was saying something. Not witch, not shifter, not a magical worker of any kind, yet she caused something inside me long dead to rise up. To come to attention. Something I'd believed under my control.

Until this moment.

The beast inside me opened an eye. Curious. Hungry.

Mine.

I shook off the thought, along with the haze that fell over my vision, swallowing down the blood thirst tightening my throat. Tonight, I needed to complete a job for Soul Management Group, the organization that handled death and reincarnation. I wasn't out seeking a blood donor or willing partner to slake my lust. Whoever this female was—*whatever* she was—I would figure it out later. Tonight, I was a killer stalking a killer.

My beast snarled with anger. I'd need to give him something to tear into in place of tasting the woman.

With Halloween a week away, store owners and groups of students from the local college had been donning costumes, allowing the creature I tracked to blend in. Dubbed The Grim Reaper, the nickname was more accurate than they realized. The serial murderer was indeed a grim, taking full advantage of the time of year to get away with stalking innocent women. It was my assignment to stop him and discover who the others were working with him.

At the corner, cold drops fell from an ancient oak, striking the unknown woman in the face and making her flinch. Glancing both ways before crossing the street, she shivered and called to the cat with a note of aggravated impatience. Her voice sent another ripple through me.

The thirst rose again, a fire ripping through me. I sipped at my wine, images of her neck bared to me, flashing through my mind. The beast sat up, eager. Clawing for its meal.

As if she sensed the danger nearby, her gaze snapped to me.

The bar still had lights on and I was the lone person at the outside tables. The sickly yellow glow from the outdoor burners partially illuminated the area, my hair damp from the drizzle but my topcoat and pants dry thanks to my magic. Pretending not to notice her stare, I wrestled with my mounting desire. She *had* to be human, the essence of her blood an anomaly. Logic ruled out any other reason.

How long had it been since one of the mundanes had caused me such a reaction?

It's her scent, I told myself. The off-ness of it. The blood in her veins might run red, but there was a thread of power—of life and death—beneath it that called to me. A living thing that I had to ignore.

The drink in front of me could not quench my thirst nor dull my attraction to her scent. My fingerless gloves toyed with the stem as I kept my focus on the glass, doing my damnedest to tame my beast. Registering her presence was one thing; the fact she continued to size me up, the weight of her scrutiny warm and malleable on my face, my body, made every restraint I had ache to be unleashed. The beast strained against its leash.

All the more reason to keep myself in check. Ignore her. Appear to be engrossed in the horrid liquid the bar passed off as fine wine.

No grim costume—her thought was full of relief.

While she had plenty to fear from that killer, the monster inside me was far more of a threat at the moment. I never lacked self-control these days, yet I discovered I was unable to resist her stare. I raised my gaze.

The eye contact caused an exhilarating current to yank taut between us. Her face was beautiful; her blue-green eyes haunted. *What has caused you so much pain?*

That tug twitched and rose, powerful as an ocean wave. I tracked the movement of her throat as she swallowed. It was all I could do not to moan.

Mine, my dragon crooned.

She seemed to draw into herself, her mind slowing. It

was so easy—too easy—to listen to her thoughts, including those about me.

Those eyes...

Mine were unusual shade of purple, a gift from my mother.

The woman's natural instinct, that survival gene we all possessed, made her jerk her gaze away and pick up her pace. As she passed the last of the burners, she saw a female standing in the shadows, watching me. Her thoughts tripped over themselves again at a rapid pace, moving as swiftly as her feet. She knew not to hesitate, yet feared for my safety, considering for one beat of her gentle, to-soft heart if she should warn me.

The corner of my mouth threatened to turn upward at that thought. I clenched my jaw and squelched it. Along with ignoring the one watching me, who was of no consequence, I shut down my libido.

A second female human approached, heels clacking on the sidewalk. Her skirt stopped well above her knees and the boots she wore jingled with each step, metal embellishments flashing. I'd been watching this one—Darcy Haynes, a local college sophomore who spent her evenings cruising the bars, rather than studying. The exact profile The Grim Reaper loved. "Hey," she said. "Chloe, right? That chem test was murder last week, wasn't it?"

Chloe. A sweet, innocent name. The chaos in Chloe's mind ramped up. As if my own semi-immortal heart had become entrained with her pounding one, I felt mine pump for the first time in a decade.

I listened carefully as she mentally tried to recall

Darcy's name. Searched her mind for anything that might allow her to save face. "Totally," she answered awkwardly. "Chemistry isn't my favorite."

So Chloe was also a student. I tucked that piece of knowledge away.

Darcey made a disgusted face, then became chipper again. "You headed to O'Malley's? Three-for-one on beers."

Potential names flitted around in Chloe's head. *Barbie? Billie?* She nodded as though it sounded like a great time. Cheap drinks, drunk college students, and mind-numbing small talk. What could be better? "I'm searching for my landlady's cat. You didn't happen to see any wayward gray tabbies, did you?"

"No, but you have to come to the parade. Everyone will be there."

"Parade?"

Darcy tilted her head, frowning. "Over on King Street for Fall Fest." This was said with a mixture of *duh* and anticipation. "I'm meeting Larson, and we're going to watch from the balcony of his dad's shop. Then we're going to O'Malley's."

Shifting to look around her, Chloe scanned the area for the feline. A Miss Pickles. "Sounds fun. Enjoy."

A pouty face was Darcy's response. "You'll come by after you find the cat?"

Chloe nodded with fake enthusiasm. "You had me at three-for-one beers."

She gave a squeal and jumped up and down. "I want you on my team for the trivia game."

Chloe's eyes narrowed. "Why is that?"

Another *duh* expression flitted over Darcey's features. "You're the smartest girl in school."

Her skirt flipped up as she trotted off to find her date, and Chloe shook her head, watching her for a moment. Her mind listed all the things Darcy didn't have to worry about. *She probably doesn't work two jobs to support herself. A Friday night getting drunk is a highlight in her college career.*

As Darcy neared the outdoor dining area, she turned back to Chloe. "Hey, do you tutor?"

"No," Chloe called quickly, trepidation rippling under her skin as she noticed me observing the interaction.

Darcy, I told her telepathically. I couldn't help myself. Something made me want to assist her. Help her. *Her name is Darcy Haynes.*

Her jaw dropped as she stared at me. She shivered visibly.

Darcy was walking backward, paying no attention to where she was headed—which was right into my table.

"Look out!" Chloe yelled.

I raised a hand and made a swift motion, a gust of my magic catching her, her body shifting away from me. She yelped, stumbling slightly, then glanced around, confused. Righting herself, she brushed at her skirt and gave an embarrassed laugh. "Hey, handsome," she said to me.

I zeroed in on my glass once more, stroking the stem. I needed her to draw out The Grim Reaper, but at that moment, she was in my way. An annoying fly, buzzing about.

"You better get going," Chloe told her, seeming to sense my impatience. "Don't want to be late."

Recovered, Darcy waved at her. "Come find me when you get there!"

Feeling Chloe's stare once more, I pointedly raised his eyes. I enjoyed the flash of challenge in her eyes and took her measure as swiftly as she did mine.

She offered a hesitant smile and everything in me went still as the night. I wanted to lick my lips, invite her over, but no—I had to stay on course, or another human would die tonight. Possibly Darcey. Forcing myself to remain frozen, I dismissed her with a cold, hard glare.

A mix of disappointment and relief speared through her. Pivoting, she took off, her mind iterating that she was tired and hungry and wanted to get back home. Jogging the last bit to the park, she disappeared from sight.

I breathed in her lingering scent and caught something else in the air—The Grim Reaper. Leaving my wine and a generous tip, I slipped into the night, sure that Chloe and I would meet again.

Get Your Next Killion Fix - Read Episode 2 now!

VISIT MY STORE

Did you know you can buy directly from me? When you do, the retailer doesn't take a cut and I can pass on the savings to YOU!

https://mistyevansbooks.com/shop

Benefits:

You can find ALL my books in one place

SAVE money

EARLY access to new releases

Special Collections, Boxed Sets, and Limited Editions

Support a small business (and support a dream!)

Why Buy Direct?

When you purchase a book by your favorite author, electronic or print, on retailer platforms, the company keeps 30-70% of the sale, leaving the author with little to no profit (after the company deducts delivery fees, taxes, and other fees).

Buying directly from the author means that more goes to them so they can keep turning out stories for you. Every published story, every book, requires cover art, editing, and hours and hours of the author's time simply to create it. Not to mention overhead costs, such as websites, newsletters, writing software, graphics programs, advertising, taxes, etc.

In addition, one of the big-name retailers requires exclusivity, and all of them have terms of service and rules and regulations that make it challenging and time-consuming for an indie author to navigate the publishing world.

Most of us would MUCH rather spend our time creating more stories for YOU, rather than trying to jump through the hoops at the retailers. Buying direct from your favorite authors (where available) helps ensure that an author you love is not subject to unexplained account closures, withholding of royalties, censorship, and other issues that can affect their livelihood.

I've experienced ALL of these. By buying direct, you help put control of my work back in my hands - and I can continue to write more.

Either way, thank you for supporting me! I understand buying direct doesn't work for everyone and even if you use the retailers to buy my books, I appreciate you!

Happy reading,

Misty
https://mistyevansbooks.com/shop

YOU'RE INVITED!

Do you have a passion for my stories?

Want more from my characters?

How about early access to ALL my new releases?

My reader community is for YOU!

Try my **VIP reader community** for a month! It's ONLY $5 - you're buying me a coffee - and in return, you get all these perks:

Writing Updates so you know what's in the works and how soon you can get it

Special Charmed Content, including episodes in my GrimVerse and Kali Sweet worlds, character interviews, alternate endings/deleted scenes, future story plot ideas, and cover reveals

Early Access to new stories - I always have multiple books in the works and I release a chapter(s) early before the stories are on retailers

Charmed Coupons for discounts to <u>my online store</u>

✦ **Pics of my pets** (all are rescues and they "help" me write and edit)!

You're invited! What are you waiting for?

I'm in! Give me more stories!

PNR & UF BY MISTY/NYX HALLIWELL

The Accidental Reaper Series

Grim & Bare It, Book 1

Reaper's Keepers, Book 2

In too Reap, Book 3

Killin' It (short story for newsletter & Ream Stories subscribers only)

The Vampire's Kiss (an exclusive short story available in Misty's Store. *Intended for mature audiences 17+*)

Grave Girl

Grave Magic

The Kali Sweet Series

Revenge Is Sweet, Kali Sweet Series, Book 1

Sweet Chaos, Kali Sweet Series, Book 2

Sweet Soldier, Kali Sweet Series, Book 3

Sweet Curse, Kali Sweet Series, Book 4

Witches Anonymous Step 1

Jingle Hells, WA Step 2

Wicked Souls, WA Step 3

Dark Moon Lilith, Witches Anonymous Step 4

Dancing With the Devil, Witches Anonymous Step 5

Devil's Due, Witches Anonymous Step 6

Dirty Deeds, Witches Anonymous Step 7

Wicked Wedding, Witches Anonymous Step 8

Soul Survivor, Moon Water Series, Book 1

Soul Protector, Moon Water Series, Book 2

COZY MYSTERIES (WRITING AS NYX HALLIWELL)

Sister Witches Of Raven Falls Mystery Series

Of Potions and Portents

Of Curses and Charms

Of Stars and Spells

Of Spirits and Superstition

Confessions of a Closet Medium Series

Pumpkins & Poltergeists

Magic & Mistletoe

Hearts & Haunts

Vows & Vengeance

Cupcakes & Corpses

Tea Leaves & Troubled Spirits

Haunted Honeymoon

Wedding Bells & Psychic Spells

Sister Witches of Story Cove Series

Cinder

Belle

Snow

Ruby

Zelle

Sister Witches of Story Cove Complete Set

***

Witchy Candy Shop Mysteries

Tricks and Treats

Candy and Creeps

Gum and Ghouls (releasing 2025)

ROMANTIC SUSPENSE & MYSTERIES

Don't want to miss a single release? Click here to join my reader list!

SEALs of Shadow Force Series

Fatal Truth

Fatal Honor

Fatal Courage

Fatal Love

Fatal Vision

Fatal Thrill

Risk

SEALS of Shadow Force Series: Spy Division

Man Hunt

Man Killer

Man Down

Covert Affairs

Covert Tactics

Covert Obsession

The SCVC Taskforce Series

Deadly Pursuit

Deadly Deception

Deadly Force

Deadly Intent

Deadly Affair, A SCVC Taskforce novella

Deadly Attraction

Deadly Secrets

Deadly Holiday, A SCVC Taskforce novella

Deadly Target

Deadly Rescue

Deadly Bounty

Deadly Betrayal

Deadly Threat

The Super Agent Series

Operation Sheba

Operation Paris

Operation Proof of Life

Operation Lost Princess

Operation Ambush

Operation Contraband

Operation Sleeping With the Enemy

The Justice Team Series (with Adrienne Giordano)

Stealing Justice

Cheating Justice

Holiday Justice

Exposing Justice

Undercover Justice

Protecting Justice

Missing Justice

Defending Justice

SCHOCK SISTERS MYSTERY SERIES w/Adrienne Giordano

1st Shock

2nd Strike

3rd Tango

The Secret Ingredient Culinary Mystery Series

The Secret Ingredient, A Culinary Romantic Mystery with Bonus Recipes

The Secret Life of Cranberry Sauce, A Secret Ingredient Holiday Novella

MEET MISTY

USA TODAY Bestselling Author Misty Evans has published over ninety novels, as well as nonfiction inspirational journals. She loves writing urban fantasy, paranormal romance, and mystery/suspense. Under her pen name, Nyx Halliwell, she also writes supernatural cozy mysteries.

When not reading or writing, she enjoys music, movies, and hanging out with her husband, twin sons, and three spoiled rescue dogs. She's a crafter at heart and has far too many projects to finish.

Visit www.mistyevansbooks.com to check out her online store and sign up for her newsletter.

LETTER FROM MISTY

Hello Beautiful Reader!

Thank you for reading this story! It is an honor and a privilege to write books for you. I'm an indie author and every fan is important to me. I pour my heart into each story and do my best to bring you an escape from the real world.

I hope you enjoyed this one, and if so, would you mind leaving a review at your favorite retailer? Or share your enjoyment of it with a friend or family member? I'd really appreciate it, and reviews help other readers find books they will love, too.

Readers are the key to my success - not a traditional publishing deal (had four), an agent (had two), or a publicity team (yep, you guessed it, had several of those as well.)

Those of you who read my books and love my characters and worlds, and who then tell others are the best of friends. I adore you and will keep writing if you keep reading!

If you'd like to learn about my other books, sales, and special promotions, please sign up for my newsletter at **www.mistyevansbooks.com**.

You'll get coupons to download starter packs for FREE, whether you love my suspense or my paranormal.

Support me directly (no retailer taking their cut), grab special edition box sets, and get new releases before they are out at retailers by visiting my store **https://mistye vansbooks.com/shop** or **joining me on Ream Stories**.

I have sales and offer NEW RELEASES early! Check it out.

Last but not least, if you enjoy clean, cozy mysteries, visit my pen name **www.nyxhalliwell.com** to see those books.

Thank you and happy reading!

Misty